HA

A St

Now she moved away, heading for the door.

I heard the shower running, then stop, heard the bathroom door open and the patter of bare feet padding into the bedroom, and the thought of her walking round stark naked stirred me.

She was lying on the bed, on her back, covered by a single sheet, every nuance of her body evident in the gentle light filtering in from the hall.

'You look like an Egyptian mummy,' I grinned from the doorway.

She turned her head and looked at me, slowly, from head to toe, then flicked back the sheet. 'Then come in here and make like an Egyptian daddy.'

Also by Stanley Morgan in *Star*

RUSS TOBIN'S BEDSIDE GUIDE TO SMOOTHER SEDUCTION

A BLOW FOR GABRIEL HORN

INSIDE ALBERT SHIFTY

THE FLY BOYS : SKY-JACKED

HARD UP

A Russ Tobin Story

Stanley Morgan

A STAR BOOK

published by

the Paperback Division of
W. H. ALLEN & Co. Ltd

A Star Book
Published in 1977
by the Paperback Division of
W. H. Allen & Co. Ltd
A Howard and Wyndham Company
123 King Street, London W6 9JG

Printed in Great Britain by
Hazell Watson & Viney Ltd, Aylesbury, Bucks.

ISBN 0 352 39559 1

CHAPTER ONE

'Aer Lingus announce the departure of their flight EI 156 to London. Passengers are requested to collect boarding cards from the check-in desk and proceed to Gate Twenty Six . . .'

The plane was going to be full, I could tell from the number of people already in the Departure Lounge, so I sidled over to the gate, hoping to get on first and find a good seat. Even on a one-hour flight I didn't fancy being stuck up front in the non-smokers among two thousand sicky kids.

I checked my watch: it was eleven o'clock and already we were ten minutes late boarding – about par for Dublin Airport. Somehow I could never get over the feeling that planes took off from Dublin only when their crews had finished their tea and not a moment sooner.

Still, I was in no particular hurry. It was a beautiful June morning and I was as free as a bird with nothing more pressing to think about than the great time I was going to have in London during the next couple of weeks.

Couple of weeks? Who knew? It might even be a couple of months before I got around to looking for another job. After what I'd been through working at *Ballytatty Castle Hotel* the past six months I was certainly in no great tearing hurry to sign on for another dose of toil. Yes, come to think of it, a two-month recuperative lay-off sounded just about right.

Ah ha! Signs of activity – a bloke in a black uniform was heading our way.

'Passengers with children first, please . . . Let the passengers with children through first! Stand back, sir, let them through.'

Here they came – hundreds of 'em. By the time they were seated there'd be standing room only in the loos.

Through the gate they went, streaming down the stairs like an army of ants, making a hell of a din.

'Right . . .' Uniform nodded at me.

I handed him my boarding card. 'On time as usual,' I observed cheerfully.

'Move on, sir, you're blocking the gate.'

I moved on, rushed down the stairs, broke into a near-run along the passenger-way and beat four other men into the plane by a head.

Two smiling airstews greeted me, bade me goodmorning and passed me into the care of two less-smiling airstews who were battling to settle the swarm of excited kids.

I took my time squeezing past a cute little stew with short dark hair and a wonderful bottom, then made my way to the back of the plane, chose the window-seat of the two seats on the right-hand side and sat down.

What, I wondered, would be my luck this flight? Same as usual, I supposed – I'd end up with a twenty-stone pig farmer from Mayo or a bishop from Ballyboring. Don't know why it is but I *never* get to sit next to a good-looking chick on a plane. The Departure Lounge could be full of Miss World candidates and I'd get lumbered with their bleeding sixty-year-old chaperone.

I watched them come aboard; the usual lot – business-men with briefcases, priests, nuns, holidaymakers. Quickly the plane filled until finally there were only three empty seats left, all at the rear, one next to me and two aisle seats opposite.

And then I saw her!

She was third in the line of people coming down the aisle, behind two men, a beautiful creature with long gleaming red hair and dreamy green eyes. My heart skipped. Come on, you guys, get sat down and let her through. She glanced up, searching for a seat, spotted the one next to me. By gum, she really had her eye on it!

The first man now swung into one of the aisle seats opposite, a row in front of mine. The next guy, a young, blond chap about my age, hesitated, considered both remaining empty seats for a moment, then made to sit in the aisle seat directly opposite me . . . she was all mine! . . . then he changed his bloody mind and flopped down next to me.

Aw, rotten hell . . . so close, so close!

I tell you, I could make a fortune placing bets on situations like this. I never get the bird!

'Sorry,' he muttered, yanking his seat belt from under my buttocks.

Not half as sorry as I am, mate.

I glanced at him, hating him, and he grinned back disarmingly. He was a very good-looking lad, blond of hair and blue of eye, with devilment in his countenance and an abundance of charm in his smile, and, despite the grief he'd just caused me, I found myself liking him.

He was smartly, casually dressed in a pale blue, open-necked shirt and dark blue slacks, and carried a patterned sports jacket and small overnight case.

Suddenly, he stood up again, threw his jacket and case into the overhead rack and sat down, this time fastening his seat-belt. Obviously he hadn't flown very much or he'd have known about the case.

'They'll have you,' I told him.

'Hm . . . who?'

'The airstews. They won't allow that case up there. They don't allow anything heavy up there in case it falls down and hits somebody on the head.'

He gave me a broadside of perfect teeth. 'Yeh, I know.'

'Oh?'

Barmy.

I lost interest in him because the red-head was reaching up to stow her denim jacket in her overhead rack and the proximity of her magnificent arse, shrink-wrapped in blue jeans, blew my brains out.

It had the same effect on my blond companion, too.

'Cor . . .' I heard him mutter.

'I'll second that,' I said.

He shot round, grinning ear-to-ear, then quickly

returned for another eyeful until she'd sat down.

'Mamma mia,' he muttered at me. 'I'd rather be in that than Wormwood Scrubs.'

'Hm hm,' I nodded. 'And perhaps now you can fully appreciate the enormity of my disappointment.'

'Hm?'

'She had her eye on the seat you're sitting in. I almost had her all the way to London.'

'No!'

'Absolutely.'

'Aw, hell, I'm sorry. Didn't even know she was behind me. That's terrible.'

'The worst.'

At that moment the little dark-haired stew hove-to, checking and closing the overhead racks. 'Sorry, sir,' she said, going up on tip-toe to haul his case out, her blouse riding high and exposing a vast expanse of exciting, sun-tanned belly, 'you'll have to put this under your seat.'

'Oh,' he said lamely, leaning forward and peering up, his nose practically in her navel. 'I'm sorry . . . I didn't realize. Here, let me . . .'

He was up behind her in a flash, pressing against her as he reached over her for his case. 'Oops, sorry, miss, it seems to be . . . stuck.'

For a good ten seconds he had her pinned to the upright of the seat as he struggled to free the case, and while he was at it he glanced down at me and beamed an evil, lascivious grin.

'Ah! I . . . think it's coming, miss . . .'

Boy, what an operator. And I thought I knew all the tricks.

'Sorry about that,' he said, blinding her with the teeth. 'I'll know where to put it next time.'

Her eyes crinkled, and with a murmured, 'I'll bet,' she waltzed off down the aisle.

'Silly me,' he tutted, sitting down again.

I shook my head. 'Beautifully executed. If there's one thing I admire it's a professional.'

'Hell, you've got to get something for your money,' he

said, re-fastening his seat-belt. 'The flight certainly isn't worth it.' He offered me his hand. 'Dennis Hopper.'

'Russ Tobin.'

'Another professional, I can tell.'

'When blokes like you give me the chance.'

'Aw, I'm really sorry about that, Russ. I reckon I owe you a drink.'

'I'll accept.'

He turned to glance at the red-head, getting a glimmer of a smile in return, then he came back to me. 'I'll make it a double. I really knackered a beautiful friendship, didn't I?'

I shook my head. 'I reckon we're quits, Dennis. I'm going to pinch your luggage-rack trick.'

He had his fags out before the 'no smoking' sign went off, a lad after my own heart.

'Thanks,' I said, giving him a light. 'What were you doing in Dublin?'

I got the grin again. 'Bird chasing. A girl I knew in London moved to Dublin and she said to drop over sometime.'

'So you dropped. I hope it was worth it.'

'Oh, boy . . . I could sleep for a year.' He shook his head in wonderment. 'She was unbelievable.'

'Looks like I'm leaving at the wrong time. Perhaps I could've looked after your interests between visits. No offence, Dennis, just a thought.'

He grinned. 'What have you been doing here?'

'My nut, mostly. I've been working at *Ballytatty Castle Hotel* in County Kildare. They specialize in package tours from the States. I was sort of Entertainments Manager – had to make sure all the lonely ladies had a jolly time.'

'Wow!' he laughed. 'How did you manage to land a job like that?'

'Through an Irish pal of mine. We played couriers together in Majorca one glorious, unforgettable summer and he called me in on this one as his assistant. He was on his knees, poor lad.'

'Boy, have I been wasting *my* time.'

'What do you do, Dennis?'

'I'm a salesman. I work the London area for an outfit called Zip Electrics. They sell a line of small appliances: food mixers, vacuum cleaners, record players, film projectors, sewing machines, that sort of thing.'

I smiled. 'Sewing machines. That takes me back. I did a spell of sewing machine selling myself a couple of years ago in Liverpool. Ritebuy Sewing Machines – a right bunch of crooks. We sold them on the "switch" method – they'd advertise a very cheap machine to get us into the house, then we'd switch the sale to a much more expensive machine . . .'

He was grinning again. 'You just described the Zip operation.'

'Oh, blimey.'

'Yeh, old Zeb's as bent as they come – he's the owner, Zebadiah Isaac Polkoski, hence the ZIP bit. He advertises the cheap Mark One appliances in local papers, then, when we get in the house, we switch to the Super De Luxe models at five times the price.'

'Are they any good?'

He shrugged. 'As good as anything made in Taiwan.'

'Oh,' I laughed. 'You just pray nothing goes wrong with them before the end of the guarantee period?'

'Huh, I reckon Polkoski won't be around that long. I reckon he's in for a quick overnight kill, then off to South America with a boatload of money.'

'Is he doing well?'

'Fantastic. He's got six salesmen and we're going flat out. The leads he gets from his newspaper advertising are amazing. I sometimes handle ten calls a day.'

'Jeez, that's terrific. What percentage do you manage to switch?'

He shrugged, 'Fifty . . . sixty percent. The Super models look terrific compared to the Mark Ones. They're not difficult to switch.'

'Is the pay good?'

'Straight commission – ten percent on the Supers, only two percent on the Mark Ones. He advertises the Mark Ones practically at cost to pull the leads in.'

'That's not a bad deal, Dennis.'

He grinned. 'Interested? He's always looking for good men. He'd snap you up if you've had experience on sewing machines.'

I shook my head. 'Nah, I had enough of the switch malarky at Ritebuy, I didn't really enjoy it. Besides, I'm not looking for work just yet. I'm going to take a few weeks off and have some fun; I've worked hard enough for the past six months.'

'Sounds like it,' he laughed. 'Will you be staying in London?'

'Yes. I'll get a room in one of those small hotels along the Brompton Road. I've still got a few quid in the bank, it should last a month or two if I keep the expenses down.'

'I envy you – having something in the bank. I can't save a bean.'

'I was lucky. A couple of years ago I earned quite a lot working as a presenter in TV commercials and was able to stick something away...'

He rounded on me. 'I thought I'd seen you before! You're the bloke who does the... whatsit...'

'White Marvel?'

'Yeh! I saw one the other night – you were chatting up a housewife about her washing...'

'Christ, are they still going out?'

'Sure! You're on a couple of times a week.'

'Oh, hell. Well, that's one idea up the shoot. I was toying with the idea of trying to do some more commercials, but if the White Marvel things are still on the air, that's it, no one else will touch me. That's why they paid me so much money in the first place, of course, to cover me for a year or two.'

'Nice kind of cover, too. So – what did you do after you made the commercials?'

'Just about everything. First I became a courier in

Majorca, then I went to Africa to do much the same sort of job on safari . . .'

'Blimey,' he laughed.

'. . . then I took off for the Bahamas, then Miami, New York, Toronto, Las Vegas, Tahiti and finally Australia. I've been right round the world in two years.'

'Wow . . .' he gasped. 'Boy, what a way to go. Did you work your way round, Russ?'

'Only a bit in Australia – for a male escort agency.'

He hooted with laughter. 'Hey, that I've got to hear about! No – start from the beginning. Tell me about Majorca.'

'You mean it?'

'Sure! I want to hear the lot. Hell, I've never been further than Dublin, and I've been thinking of having a go at something abroad myself. Maybe this will help.'

I shrugged. 'Okay, they're your ears . . .'

Well, I started, and he became so interested, bombarded me with so many questions, that we were dropping for Heathrow before I'd even got out of Africa.

'London already?' he frowned. 'Can't be, we've only just taken off.'

'I've been rattling on for an hour, Dennis.'

'Aw heck . . .' He suddenly brightened. 'Hey . . . how are you getting into London?'

I shrugged. 'Bus, I suppose.'

'I'll give you a lift – my car's at the airport.'

'Terrific, thanks a lot.'

'Don't thank me, I've got to hear the end of this, it's fantastic.'

I believed him. He hadn't looked at the red-head once.

CHAPTER TWO

His car, a canary-yellow Spitfire, reflected his personality perfectly – fast and cheeky. He gunned it down the ramps of the multi-storey car park to the ticket-office, handed over a couple of quid, then was away with a squeal of rubber, showing off a bit. But for all that I felt he was a good driver.

On the dual-carriageway into London, with the hood down and the wind in our faces, he kept the speed reasonable so we could talk without having to bellow at each other, though I detected that normally anything less than ninety would be agony for him.

'Nice car, Dennis.'

'Thanks. I sweated blood for it. It's not new but it's all mine – I've just made the last payment on it, thanks to Zip.'

'Do you live at home?'

He laughed derisively. 'Not likely. I've got a room in a crazy boarding-house in Balham. The owners are Italian and the place stinks of cheese and spaghetti, but I like it. They're all nutters there but nice with it.'

I grinned. 'Any birds?'

'Yeh! There's a belter just moved in, next floor up. Fantastic figure, really stacked – don't know what she does but she can try me for starters! Real sexy-looking piece, very dark skin and beautiful eyes. I'll have to do something about her now I'm back.'

'Nothing like having it on tap, son – saves you a fortune in petrol.'

'Damn right,' he laughed.

After a moment he got back to the subject of jobs. 'What did you do before sewing machines, Russ?'

'I did a spell of penal servitude in a dump of an office

near Liverpool docks – Wainwright's Building Supplies. I died an agonized death every morning.'

He nodded. 'I know it. My parents shoved me in Wandsworth Town Hall when I left school, and I aged forty years in the first week. I got fired the second week.'

'Why?'

He laughed. 'For writing "knickers" across the Rates Ledger. I couldn't stand another minute of it.'

'What did you do then?'

'Oh . . . a number of things. Stacked tins in a supermarket, pumped petrol in a gas station, sold men's underwear in Harrods . . . just kept moving, trying to find something that interested me. Then I found Zip.'

'What would you really like to do?'

'Sail my own yacht round the Caribbean,' he laughed. 'I should have been born rich.'

'Amen to that! My sentiments exactly.'

'At least you've been round the world. I reckon it's time I started earning some real money.'

'Maybe you should try TV commercials; you'd knock 'em cold in the Martini ads. If you like, I'll give you the name of my agent.'

'Nah, don't be daft, I couldn't act to save myself.'

'You think so? So what do you do every time you flog a Zip Super appliance? You give the poor unsuspecting housewife a song-and-dance act, don't you?'

He threw back his head and laughed. 'Yeh, true, but that's different.'

'Not a bit of it, Yeh, I'll bet you really give them the works, too: Dennis Hopper – the answer to the lonely housewife's prayer.'

'Who – me? Nothing like that's ever happened to me. I reckon it's all salesmen's bull.'

'Oh?'

He shot a glance at me. 'It happened to you? Really? Hey, tell me about it.'

'Dennis, I haven't even finished telling you about Africa yet! It'll take me a week at this rate and we're at Hammersmith already.'

'That's okay, I've got nothing else to do until three o'clock. Oh, sorry . . . didn't mean to sound pushy. You probably want to get settled in by yourself.'

I shook my head. 'Nope. Help me find a hotel if you'd like to.'

'Terrific! How about some lunch afterwards in Soho? One of the blokes in my boarding house works at an Italian caff in Greek Street and he always knocks a chunk off the bill.'

'You're on. Let's find a place to dump these cases and I'm all yours.'

We found the *Excelsior,* a small, newly-decorated hotel in a street off the Brompton Road.

A somewhat formal young stiff in a morning suit looked me over carefully before offering me the register. 'How long will you be staying, Mister Tobin?'

'I'm not sure, probably a minimum of a week, though. I'll let you know.'

He cleared his throat awkwardly. 'I regret, sir, I must ask you for a deposit of thirty pounds – company policy.'

I frowned at him. 'Bit unusual, isn't it?'

He spread his hands. 'Alas, we have had several recent cases of dishonoured cheques, and the management has been forced to . . .'

'Yes, all right.' I got out my cheque book.

'The city is teeming with tourists,' he went on apologetically, 'not all as honourable as one might wish, I'm afraid. It is most regrettable that the old standards of trust cannot be . . . ah, thank you, sir.'

He inspected my cheque with the fervour of an FBI bloke who'd stumbled on a counterfeit hundred-dollar bill, then broke out in a relieved smile. 'Ah, a local bank . . . Piccadilly Circus. Splendid.' He turned to get my key and dangled it at me. 'Room 222, second floor front. Do enjoy your stay with us, sir. The porter will take your luggage up for you when he returns.'

'Don't bother, we can manage. We're in a bit of a hurry.'

'As you wish, sir.'

Dennis and I squeezed into the tiny lift and punched the appropriate button.

'Trusting soul,' he observed.

'Yeh, well, I suppose he's got a point. There must be more rubber bouncing around London in cheque form than on Dunlop's test track. And what better value than a week in a hotel? You run up a nifty bill, pay with a dud cheque as you book out, and move into another hotel. You could live like a lord for years if they didn't insist on a deposit.'

'I wouldn't have the nerve to try it.'

'Me, neither.'

The room was fine – neat, clean, with a view over the tree-lined street. With Dennis' help I unpacked my gear in a matter of minutes and within a few more minutes we were on our way to Soho.

'I really dig London in summer,' he said, breathing deeply as we drove past Hyde Park, as though he had a hope of inhaling anything but traffic fumes.

'Me, too. I shall never forget my first summer down here. I chummed up with a lad who knew a couple of Soho strippers who had a pad off Park Lane . . .' I shook my head and laughed. 'Boy, I really thought I'd never live to see Christmas.'

'That's something *else* you've got to tell me about! We'd better make this lunch *and* dinner.'

'I'm not sure all this excitement is good for you, Dennis. I think I'd better stick to my life story in Wainwright's office before I stepped out into the wicked world.'

'You do and I'll get Bruno to put triple garlic in your meat balls and stymie your love-life for a month.'

'Okay, okay – but I'll not be held responsible for the consequences. You're taking this too much to heart.'

'Damn right,' he grinned. 'You've got me going now. I reckon this is the push I've needed for a long time. Twenty-five years old and I've never been further than Dublin . . .

disgraceful. It's about time I did something about it.'

'Well, the first step is the hardest. After that it becomes almost habit.'

'Yeh,' he nodded.

His tone of fervour made me glance at him. He was staring straight ahead with an expression of glazed intensity and I could tell his thoughts were a million miles from Piccadilly. I smiled to myself, remembering my own excitement at the prospect of venturing into the great unknown, a prospect that still excited me, despite my experiences around the world. Once a traveller, always a traveller, I guess. Get the bug in your blood and it's there for life.

We managed to find a parking space in Soho Square, and from there it was only a short walk down Greek Street to the restaurant. It wasn't much of a place, barely a dozen tables, but it smelled appetizing and looked clean.

Bruno, a young, diminutive Italian with a beaming smile and bandy legs, greeted Dennis effusively, shook my hand vehemently, and led us to a rear table. And there, for the next hour, over a mountain of spaghetti and a bottle of Chianti, I continued to pour excitement and unrest into Dennis' willing ear.

I'd just finished telling him of my incredible adventure with Stud Ryder and the delectable Delphi on Paradise Island and was about to proceed to my torrid experience with the man-eating Malinda when, suddenly, he glanced at his watch and uttered a desolate groan.

'What's the matter?' I asked.

'It's two-thirty. I've got to be back at Zip at three. The boss has four leads for me this afternoon.'

'Then go-go.'

He heaved a sigh. 'I don't want to. Suddenly I've lost my appetite for flogging food mixers.'

'Now, now, Dennis, you mustn't let my yarns upset you. You can't afford to stop working.'

'Damn right,' he grumbled, unimpressed with the argument.

I sympathized with him, knowing too well what he was suffering.

'What are you doing tonight?' I asked him.

He shrugged. 'Nothing.'

'All right – why not come round to the hotel and have a beer or something? Maybe take a drive and ogle the girls?'

He brightened. 'Terrific! What time?'

'Seven-ish?'

'Fantastic.' He signalled Bruno for the bill and while we were waiting, he fished a business card out of his pocket and scribbled a number on the back.

'This is my home number – in case something comes up and you can't make it.'

'Okay . . . but I'm not expecting anything to come up.'

He grinned. 'You never know your luck.'

Bruno arrived with the bill and I plucked it off the plate before Dennis could get to it.

'Hey! . . .' he protested.

'This is on me, you're paying for the petrol.'

The bill came to five pounds sixty. I got my money out and counted off six one-pound notes. It was all I had.

'Hey, you're skint,' protested Dennis.

'Only momentarily. I didn't have time to get to the bank in Dublin; I'll walk down to Piccadilly and get some now.'

'You sure? I've got plenty.'

'Positive. I've got to get some more anyway.'

'I'll drop you off, then.'

'Where does Zip Electrics hang out?'

'Kennington – near the Oval.'

'Then Piccadilly's out of your way. Don't worry, Dennis, I'll walk down.'

'Well, if you're sure.'

We parted outside the restaurant, Dennis turning up towards Soho Square, me heading down to Shaftesbury Avenue, then along to Piccadilly Circus.

It felt good to be back in London, to be strolling again through familiar territory, rubbing shoulders with the crowd, enjoying the characters and the girls in summer dresses. No city in the world offers more eyeball delight in that direction than London in high summer.

I reached Piccadilly Circus, my progress slowed to a shuffle by the crowds of shoppers and tourists filling the pavements, and finally entered the cool quiet of Thingy's Bank with a sense of relief.

I glanced along the line of tellers' cages, looking for a familiar face, but they'd all gone. In their place, however, was a cute little pigeon with blonde curly hair, captivating dimples and a mind-blowing bosom, and, being ever-ready to mix business with pleasure, I headed for Miss Esme Cutler.

She looked up and hit me with the dimples. 'Hi.' She sounded American.

'Hello.' I waggled my cheque book at her. 'I have an account here . . . Russ Tobin. I'd like to cash fifty pounds.'

'Sure.' She reached for a counter withdrawal form and slid it to me. 'I haven't seen you in here before, have I?'

'Alas, no. I've been abroad for a couple of years. I've an idea I'm going to be making up for it in the next few months, though. I'm taking a well-earned holiday, so keep your counting finger at the ready.'

'Okay, Big Spender.'

'Perhaps you'd care to help me spend some of it?'

'Nice thought, but I doubt my fiancé would share it.'

'Oh.' I pointed at her name sign. 'That . . . is criminally deceptive. It ought to read "Miss Esme Cutler – Engaged".'

'I'll see to it,' she laughed, taking my withdrawal slip.

She slid off her stool and moved to a rack of statements some distance behind the counter. She was wearing a black tailored skirt and white blouse of the simplest design, yet managed to transform it into an ensemble of such bewitching sexiness I suddenly felt quite faint with desire. So overcome was I, in fact, that it was some moments before I realized she was taking an inordinately long time perusing my bank statement. Then, instead of returning to the counter, she made off across the office to confer with a small, fat, bald bloke with glasses and a permanent scowl.

What, I wondered, could be wrong?

Scowl looked up and peered at me over his glasses, then said something to Esme who started back towards me, her cheeks no longer dimpled, her expression, if anything, downright glum – as though she had bad news to impart and hated having to do it.

Anxiously I awaited her arrival, mystified yet curious. What *could* be wrong?

'Mr Tobin, I . . .' she said hesitantly, sliding her incredible bottom onto that lucky old stool. 'I'm afraid I can't cash fifty pounds for you . . . you're already overdrawn.'

I stared at her. 'Pardon?'

She slid the statement to me, pointing to the final balance. 'It's not much, I admit, only two pounds forty-two, but I'm afraid I can't cash any more for you.'

Now I was gaping . . . down at the statement . . . up at her. 'I . . . there must be a mistake! I should have five hundred pounds in there! Someone else must have been drawing it out!'

'Oh dear . . .' she said, obviously perplexed. 'Are you certain? Have you been checking your statements as you got them?'

'Um . . . well, no. I've been abroad, you see. I haven't had a statement for . . .'

'But they have been sent out, Mr. Tobin. Didn't you leave a forwarding address?'

'Well . . . no, not exactly. They've been going to my home in Liverpool and . . . But I *couldn't* have spent all that money!'

'Have you been keeping an accurate record of withdrawals on your cheque-book stubs?'

'I . . . er, no. Because I've been withdrawing it in drafts and things overseas.'

'Perhaps that's where you've gone astray? I think you'd better have a word with Mr Roach, our accountant, and sort it all out.'

'Yes . . . I think I'd better.'

She let me in through a side-door and took me across

to Roach's desk. He was on the phone and waved me into an upright chair. With little else to do I followed Esme's undulating bum all the way back to her counter, reluctantly relinquishing the spectacle as Roach came off the phone.

'Now . . .' he grunted, settling in for an enjoyable third-degree, 'what's all this, Mr Tobin?'

'It's a bank statement,' I said, jollying up the moment.

'And not a very pretty one,' he sniffed, jollying it down again.

For a long, pregnant moment he perused the computed proof of Tobin's rise and fall, during which time I felt my attention once more magnetically drawn to Esme Cutler's studendous posterior, perched cheekily on its stool, its voluptuous symmetry dissipating my concern over mere money matters and diverting my mind along highways and byways of spectacular carnal speculation. Unbelievable . . .

'You haven't been getting it, then, Mr Tobin,' said Roach, shattering my despicable reverie.

'Hm?'

'Your bank statement – you haven't been getting it?'

'Oh! Er . . . no. No, I've been abroad for a couple of years.'

'It *has* been posted out at regular intervals,' he insisted, 'to the address you supplied to us. The bank cannot be held responsible if it wasn't forwarded to you.'

'I'm not blaming the bank.'

'Oh? Oh.' He relaxed a bit, became paternal, tutted as he perused my statement and shook his head. 'You've spent an awful lot of money in the past year, Mr Tobin. Even the deepest well will eventually dry up if it's not replenished.'

'I was travelling through countries where I wasn't allowed to work.'

'Oh? Where were they?'

'The Bahamas, the United States, Tahiti, Australia . . .'

His eyes popped. 'Well, of course that explains it, doesn't it. You can't expect to go right round the world *and* have money in the bank. Might I suggest you've been a little improvident, Mr Tobin . . . that you should have returned home before your money ran out?'

'But I didn't know it had run out, did I? That surely is why I'm sitting here?'

His mouth thinned. 'Then perhaps "irresponsible" might be a more fitting charge, Mr Tobin. Running a bank account is a responsibility not to be taken lightly.'

Good God, I was only two pounds forty-two overdrawn. He made it sound as though I'd just nosed ahead of the National Debt.

'However,' he continued, clearing his throat authoritatively, 'what is done is done, what is spent is spent. What we now have to ascertain is how you intend running the account in the future. What do you have in mind?'

'A . . . small overdraft?' I ventured.

His brow came down with a clang. 'How small?'

I shrugged. 'Enough to see me through until I can find a job.'

His brow shot up again like a roller blind. 'You haven't got a job!'

'No.'

'Oh dear, oh dear . . .' He looked about him, bewildered, as though his desk had just disappeared before his very eyes. 'Oh *dear*, oh dear . . . Er . . . how about Social Security?'

I shook my head. 'I didn't keep my stamps up.'

He winced, agonized. I could see I was hurting his feelings. 'Mr Tobin, I . . .' he sighed despondently. 'Do you have any collateral?'

I had to think. 'No.'

'Nothing? Nothing at all? How about life insurance?'

'No.'

'Good heavens. How about shares . . . property . . . jewellery?'

'Ah – yes!' I said eagerly, shooting back my cuff. 'This watch!'

He frowned at it. 'How much did it cost?'

My enthusiasm waned, remembering. 'Eight pounds. I lost my good one in Miami.'

Hè expelled air like a punctured lilo and shook his head again. 'Mr Tobin, I really don't see how . . .'

'Mr Roach, I *need* that fifty pounds,' I insisted, finger-stabbing the withdrawal slip. 'I've got to pay for a hotel room . . . for food. I'm flat broke!'

He was still shaking his turnip head. 'Mr Tobin, times are hard! The bank is under strict directives from the Government to restrict all existing overdrafts and forbid any new ones! Not only are we not *lending* any new money, but we are calling in existing loans! The situation is very serious!'

'Sure,' I nodded, 'and lending me fifty quid is going to bring the country crashing down.'

'Obviously not,' he retorted stiffly, 'but a Government directive is a Government directive and must be obeyed. In fact . . .' he gave an embarrassed cough, '. . . regarding your overdrawn balance . . .'

I stared at him. 'You need the two pounds forty-two back!'

He shifted uneasily. 'Well . . . as soon as you can manage it.'

I bellowed a laugh, startling everyone in the room, and stood up. 'By jove,' I exclaimed, clenching a fist, 'little did I realise that one day I would hold the fate of Great Britain in the palm of my hand. What power! What terrifying power! I can either withhold that two pounds forty-two and watch, gleefully, as the country sinks slowly into economic oblivion . . . or pay it back and witness old England's immediate restoration to all her former glory! Well, it's not a decision to be taken without some thought, Mr Roach, I'll have to let you know next week.'

'No need to be facetious, Mr Tobin,' he sniffed, getting to his feet.

'Oh, really? Got a home to go to tonight, have you, Mr Roach? I haven't.'

'I cannot be held responsible either for Government directives *or* for the handling of your account,' he started, heading for the door. 'No need to take it out on me. Perhaps in future you'll be more careful with your money, keep a closer eye on your expenditure.'

He opened the door and I ambled through, giving him a grin. 'Think of me curled up on the Embankment tonight, Mr Roach, wrapped in newspapers. Hey, you wouldn't have seven pence for an Evening Standard, would you?'

He closed the door behind me.

I waved adieu to the lovely Cutler as I passed her grille. 'Bye, love, see you in the soup line.'

'Here,' she whispered. 'Are you really flat broke?'

'No,' I lied, stirred by her concern and stupendous chest measurement. 'Between you and me I've got a million ICI shares, but I can't bear the thought of breaking into them.'

'No, seriously! I could lend you something if you're desperate.'

I was quite overcome. 'What a lovely thought. But no thanks, Esme, I'll be all right, I've got a few contacts. I'll be back in the black in no time – probably working down a coal mine.'

She laughed. 'Well, if you're sure.'

'You're a doll. See you.'

I left the bank in a daze, completely biffed by shock, and, with no precise destination in mind, crossed Regent Street and began wandering along Piccadilly Street towards Green Park.

I could *not* be broke. I simply could *not* be absolutely, totally penniless! It was ridiculous! I was Russ Tobin, the chap who'd earned a small fortune in telly, who'd tucked it away in the bank instead of squandering it, who'd . . . yeh, who'd bought air tickets from Africa to the Bahamas, from Toronto to Las Vegas, Las Vegas to Tahiti to Australia, Australia to England.

I heaved a despondent sigh. I *was* bloody broke.

Passing the Jolyon caff, I paused, the realization now striking me that I could not afford to buy even the meanest tuppenny bun in the window.

Suddenly I was overwhelmed with panic. I had to get some money – fast! My God, the hotel! The cheque I'd given them would bounce! I'd be chucked out on the street . . . maybe even arrested!

I walked on, mind racing, clawing desperately for a solution. Dennis! He'd lend me a quid or two. I'd phone him at Zip Electrics and . . .

How was I going to phone him? I didn't even have two lousy pence for a phone call!

Aw, this was preposterous.

Numb with shock, I wandered on, seeing nothing, hearing nothing around me, so engrossed in my dilemma that I didn't realise I'd entered Green Park until the filthy old tramp on the next seat spoke to me.

'Excuse me, old boy . . .'

'Hm?'

I looked up, surprised to find I was in the park, then glanced left and right, wondering where the refined voice had come from.

'I say, would you have the time, old chap?'

I stared at him, at this bundle of foul rags, his voice as improbable as a quack from a dog.

'The time, old bean – would you have it on you?'

'Er . . . yes. It's . . . quarter to four.'

'Ah, time for tea. Thank you.'

He stirred himself, gathered up his belongings – a crumpled newspaper and a plastic carrier bag – and stood up, the effort quite exhausting him. Stretching to ease his stiffness, he tottered a few steps in my direction, then paused to get his breath back.

'*Wonderful* day,' he exclaimed expansively, inhaling deeply then erupting in a coughing fit. 'Oh, dear, I *must* stop doing that.' The spasm over, he gazed slowly around the park, nodding to himself with satisfaction. 'Wonderful . . . wonderful.'

I was damn glad he was standing down wind. He looked as though he'd slept the night in a pig trough.

'*What is this life if, full of care . . .*' he began to recite. '*We have no time to stand and stare . . .*' Then, with startling suddenness and a complete change of thought, he plunged his hand deep into his plastic bag and frantically rummaged among its contents with the panicked urgency of someone checking the whereabouts of his wallet.

I never did discover what he was looking for, because in the next breath he abandoned the search and broke into a little jig, turned round three times, arms outstretched, cackling insanely, and slobbering down his beard.

Nutty as a bar of Cadbury's Brazil, poor bugger.

Suddenly he stopped and regarded me quizzically. 'Would you have a cigarette, dear chap?'

I got my packet out. There were just two left. I took one out and gave it to him. 'I'm a bit short, I'm afraid.'

He plucked it from my fingers and tucked it into the breast pocket of his despicable coat. 'You, sir, are a gentleman.' He looked at me intently through ancient eyes buried deep in wrinkled flesh. 'Do I detect a certain melancholy, sir? Would I be addressing another victim of life's indefatigable cruelty?'

I smiled. 'Not quite as serious as that. A temporary financial set-back, that's all.'

He gave a start, cocking his head. 'Hungry?'

Before I could answer he plunged his hand into his treasure trove again and brought out a half-eaten, brown-fleshed apple. 'Have lunch with me. I have already feasted majestically.'

My stomach churned. 'No, really. I've had lunch . . . really.'

He gave a shrug, bit voraciously into the apple and dropped the remainder back into the bag. 'Then, dear sir, I bid you farewell.'

'Goodbye.'

He turned away but paused, came back, and thrust his newspaper into my hands. 'A small recompense,' then he was off. I watched his progress, watched him rifle a garbage bin, re-equip himself with a newspaper, pocket half a banana and a bit of sandwich, then totter off across the grass.

Yes, I thought, and I'd be looking like that by the end of the week if I didn't get my hands on some dibs.

I glanced at the paper he'd given me and wished I hadn't.

Banner headlines proclaimed, 'Storm Over Huge Losses In State Industries'. The more I read, the sicker I got. Here was I, unable to borrow a lousy fifty quid because of a Government clamp-down on bank loans, while simultaneously *they* were pouring billions down the drain through chronic mismanagement of nationalized industries.

What a bloody silly world.

I turned the page, noting that the thousand million pound Concorde project was in jeopardy because of yet another strike, that we'd given away our latest ground-to-air missile to the Americans for nothing, that we'd lost a four hundred million pound Arabian desalination project to the Germans because of lax delivery dates, and that Mps' salaries were going up by ten pounds a week.

Yes, I could see the justice of clamping down on overdrafts, the arrogant, stupid sods.

I turned another page. 'Dairyman Milks Social Security of £20,000' struck my eye, while further down the page, 'I will do what has to be done, regardless of sacrifice, to put the country back on its feet,' said the Chancellor. 'Even though it may entail a further burden of taxation.'

That's the way, son – sock it to us. Just make sure there are enough plastic carrier bags to go round, that's all. We'll all be ragged-arsed tramps by the end of the year, the way things seem to be going. Well, the sooner the better – there's a certain comfort in knowing you can't sink any lower.

I flung the Happy Sheet aside and returned to my problem. Damn it, I *had* to find two pence to call Dennis! The ludicrousness of the situation almost made me laugh out loud. Two lousy pence! A coin of such insignificance it was hardly worth carrying its weight in your pocket.

I gazed around me, at the hundreds of people sitting in deckchairs and sunning themselves on the grass. The chances were that every single one of them had a two pence piece in their pockets they'd be glad to part with if they knew my plight.

So – what are you going to do about it, Tobin? They're not mind-readers. No one's going to stroll over and offer you two pence. Get over there and plead your case.

It wasn't easy. I'd never asked anyone for anything in my life. Gawd, when I think of the money I'd given away to bums, beggars, winos and layabouts who'd tapped me in the street. Surely it wasn't asking too much to get a measly two pence back when I desperately needed it?

Gird your loins, Tobin, and get cracking, otherwise you'll be sitting here when the park closes.

All right, now let's see . . . who's a likely candidate for a soft touch? Ah ha! Sitting over there in a deckchair, a kindly-looking old bloke, feeding birdseed to a flock of pigeons. He'd be a cert.

I got up and sauntered over, big smile, bags of charm.

'Er, excuse me, sorry to intrude, but I . . . I find myself in a most embarrassing situation. I need to make an important phone call but I've left all my money in the office! Ha ha! Stupid, I know, but I . . . I wonder if you could kindly *lend* me two pence? I really do hate asking you, but . . . I'd be most happy to take your name and address and send it back to you . . . ridiculous situation . . . so sorry to . . .'

He beamed up at me happily, holding out his bag of seed. 'Da da! Vraskich drobne vura grabkit gobglut . . . da da!'

Oh, fucking hell . . .

'Nein nein,' I sighed, shaking my head. 'You speaka da Eeenglisch?'

'Da da!' he nodded, pushing the bag at me. 'Drasme novitch skoplit plonski!'

I refused his offer and moved on.

Ah! Nice old dear, also sitting in a deckchair, reading a letter, her expression benign, smiling, like she'd just had good news.

I strolled over. 'Excuse me, madam, I hate to intrude...'

She gave a start, her eyes narrowed, filled with suspicion, fear, hatred. 'Stracke handen utgangarna sag *fuk*tighet!' she spat. 'Narma sig staden en *gaspning* ock sjalvmordsstatistiken!'

Jesus, aren't there any English in England any more!

'Keep your wig on, mother,' I muttered, moving off fast.

Shaking from the encounter, I made for the gate, now loath to approach anyone else in case they called a cop or hit me with their handbag. What a crazy, preposterous situation. Surely there was *one* Good Samaritan in the whole of London?

Yes, there was. He was coming towards me, dressed to the nines, ebony cane wielded with a flourish, rich as Croesus.

'Excuse me, sir . . .' I smile disarmingly. 'A ludicrous situation . . . I am in desperate need of two pence for a telephone call and unfortunately have left all my money in the office...'

Without slowing, he wagged a finger at me. ' "Neither a lender nor a borrower be", my boy . . . William Shakespeare.' And flashed past me.

' "Cunt" . . . D. H. Lawrence,' I muttered, and wandered on.

'Excuse, pliz...'

I looked up. It was a lovely Indian bird in a blue and gold sari, with a red tiddly-wink stuck on her forehead and a ruby in the side of her nose.

'Hello,' I said.

She unfolded a smile of dazzling radiance. 'You pliz tell me way to Fuck Street?'

Eh?

'Pardon?'

'Fuck Street.'

'Well, I...'

By gum, you never know the minute, do you?

I gave a cough. 'Well, there are plenty of them in Soho,

love . . . there's Greek Street, Frith, Dean. They're all pretty hot stuff.'

She frowned so hard her tiddly-wink almost fell off. 'Pliz? You don't know Fuck Street?'

She brought her hand from beneath the folds of her sari and offered me a piece of paper. 'Read, pliz?'

I took it, read it, burst out laughing. 'Oh . . . *Fox* Street! Fox Street, Canning Town, E.16. Oh, you're miles away from it, angel, you'll have to get a bus or a Tube train.'

'Oh? Not taxi?'

'It's a very long way. It'll cost you a fortune.'

She shrugged unconcernedly. 'That okay. I get taxi. Sank you.'

Off she toddled.

'Hey!'

She turned back.

'Look . . . sorry to have to ask you, but would you have two pence for a phone call? I've left my money in the office and . . .'

'Two pence?'

'Yes, you know . . . a little coin.'

She smiled regretfully and shook her head. 'Sorry, I have no coins.' This time her other hand appeared from under her sari, clutching a twenty-pound note. 'This is all I have.'

'Shame.'

Blooming marvellous, isn't it? Well, thank God for them, we *need* them. And the sooner they do buy Britain the better, our living standard will rocket overnight.

I strolled on towards the gate, wondering how long it would take me to walk to Zip Electrics in Kennington, and was just pasing through the gate when a young lad, a dirty-faced urchin, came hurtling round the fruit stall and ran straight into me.

'Owww!' I gasped.

I lifted him off my right foot and, in setting him down, heard the joyous tinkle of coins in his pocket. I stared down at him. 'Hey . . . you've got money!'

He glowered up at me. 'I didn't pinch it!'

I dropped into a crouch. 'I didn't say you did. What's your name?'

His eyes darted left and right, furtive as a fox. 'William Harold Warner.'

'Listen, William . . . how would you like to swop two pence for ten pence?'

His eyes narrowed even narrower. 'What's the catch?'

'The catch is . . . I haven't got the ten pence.'

He made a lunge to escape but I caught his arm. 'Now, hang on, let me finish. Please!' He relaxed a bit – had to or I'd have broken his arm. 'Listen, I'm not trying to con you . . . Heavens, you don't think I'd pinch a kid's money, do you?'

'Yes.'

'I . . . oh.'

'Me dad does.'

'Well, *I* wouldn't, but I'm in a bit of a fix. I need two pence to make a phone call – just one tiny twopenny piece, that's all. Now, if you'd lend me two pence, I'll take your name and address and send you ten pence through the post . . .'

'Garn,' he sneered. 'Pull the other one, it's got bells on.'

'I will – honest! Cross my heart and hope to die.'

'That's a load of old cobblers . . . don't mean a thing.'

I sighed dispiritedly. What have we done to our children?

'It does with me, William,' I said earnestly. 'I wouldn't let you down.'

His contemptuous sneer undiminished, he asked, 'Got anything to sell?'

'Hm.' I hadn't thought of that! 'Like what?'

'Got any fags?'

My hand flew to my pocket, to my last precious, life-giving snout . . . then it came out again, empty.

'No,' I said.

'Why not?'

'You're too young.'

'I've bin smokin' since I wus five.'

'That's why you're so small. Hey . . . tell you what I have got!'

'What?'

I rummaged desperately through my pockets, pulling out an address book, comb, lighter, half a packet of Polo mints . . .

'Mints?' I suggested.

'Don't like 'em.'

. . . a used bus ticket, a crumpled brochure for Ballytatty Castle, a key-chain . . .

'That!' He pounced.

'The key-chain?'

'Yus, I'll give you two pence for that.'

'But it's brand new – cost me nearly a quid!'

He shrugged. 'Take it or leave it.'

The little . . . I yanked off the keys and handed it to him. 'Here.'

He plunged his hand into his trouser pocket and hauled out a fistful of coins. Christ, he must have had a quids-worth!

'Where did you get all that!'

He grinned diabolically. 'People give it to me. I tell 'em I'm lost and they give me money for bus fare to get 'ome. Here y'are . . .'

'William, that key-chain's worth a lot more than two pence . . . fair's fair.'

'An'a deal's a deal,' he said, stuffing the money back in his pocket.

I could not dispute the truth of it.

'Okay – go on, push off.'

He pushed.

I watched him go, saw him select his first victim, put on a forlorn, little-boy-lost expression and shuffle up to an elderly woman in a deckchair. By God, it worked. Out came her handbag, over went the money, then he was off, stalking his next sucker. By the time he was thirty he'd be buying the Dorchester back from the Arabs.

Well, I had my own problems to think about.

Clutching my two pence piece as though it was the

Kohinor Diamond, I approached the brace of telephone kiosks just beyond the fruit stall and got lucky – a man was just coming out of one as I arrived.

'Is it working?' I asked him.

He beamed a smile. 'Gras podgup yak dribble kruk smelsbit!' he nodded eagerly.

'Danker shane . . . merci buckets . . . arri viderchi.'

I entered the kiosk. By gum, he was right, it did smelsbit. I picked up the receiver and held it to my ear while looking round for the dog that must have crawled in there and died a month ago . . . then became aware of the severed wire dangling around my chin.

I smashed the receiver back in its cradle and yanked open the door, colliding with a huge, brutal-looking woman who was determined to get in.

'Iss goot?' she demanded.

'Nein, love, iss cutski.' I made scissors with my fingers.

She breathed a garlic sigh in my face and, while I was recovering, beat me to the queue lining up for the second kiosk.

'Bloody marvellous, isn't it?' I muttered to the bloke running the fruit stall.

He gave me a grin, 'You wanna nip over to the Continent and phone, mate, the bleedin' place must be empty. They're all over 'ere taking advantage of our shrinkin' pound. LOVerly strawbrEEEEES! Only nineteen guineas a punnet! Mortgage yer 'ouse and get yer strawbrees 'ere!' He slid me a wink. 'They'd pay it, too, silly bastards. Hey up, 'ere comes a likely lad . . .'

An Arab in flowing white robes, tailed by three women wearing yashmaks, hove-to.

'Strawbrees, your Highness?' wheedled the Cockney, taking the piss. 'Loverly English strawbrees . . . fresh in from California this mornin'.'

Grinning, the Arab bought twelve punnets, lumbered the women with them, and strolled on.

'There 'e goes – orf to make a bid for Hyde Park, I'll be bound,' cracked Honest Ed. 'Wish he'd make a bid for this bleedin' stall. He could have it for three pounds ten and an oil change. STRAWBS! they're loverly . . . only two million piastres a punnet! Load your camels 'ere!'

Frau Goering, who had slipped into the kiosk during this exchange, now exploded out of it, muttering to herself.

'Iss goot?' I asked her, but only got a filthy look in return. I stepped in, keeping the door ajar with my foot until I checked the instrument was working, then, asphyxiated by her garlic aftermath, dialled the number on Dennis' business card.

The voice that answered was unadulterated delight, soft as a pony's nose, deep, rich and fruity. She didn't give a name, just repeated the number.

'Er . . . Zip Electrics?' I asked.

'At your service,' she breathed seductively. 'What may I do for you?'

Oh, baby . . .

'My name is Tobin . . . Russ Tobin . . .'

'*Won*derful. You sound just the man I'm looking for.'

'Hm . . . ?' What *had* I stumbled on?

'You're calling about the vacancy?'

'Vacancy?'

'On the sales team?' she said a little hesitantly.

I laughed. 'No – regretfully. No, I'm trying to contact Dennis Hopper.'

'Oh! Oh, I'm sorry! We've got an ad. in the paper for salesmen, you see . . . sorry about that.'

'My pleasure. Is Dennis there?'

'I'll have to go into the warehouse and see. Will you hold on?'

To you, love, any day of the week. By the cringe, what had Dennis got himself down there? She sounded fantastic.

I visualized her sitting at her switchboard: tall, slender, blindingly blonde, her skirt riding high, exposing a pair of fabulous thighs. I wouldn't mind applying for the job just to get an eyeful of her. So thinking, my imagination soared. I saw myself entering the Reception. She'd be there in her little office, waiting . . .

'Hi . . .'

'Hi. I'm Tobin.'

'Fantastic. Come in, take a seat. I have to check your qualifications.'

'For what?'

'For this, you dope.'

She'd be on me in a flash, her tongue playing pistons down my throat. She'd break away, wild-eyed, breathless. 'Christ, you can kiss.'

I'd give her a lazy smile. 'What's next on the agenda?'

Her hand would drop to my fly. 'This, you big, gorgeous brute . . .'

' 'Ere! Are you goin' to be in there all bleedin' day!'

I shot round, coming face-to-face with a wrinkled hag who'd opened the door.

'Are you usin' that thing or just standin' there dreamin'?'

'Hello . . .' cooed Cutie in my ear. 'I'm afraid Dennis won't be back until five-thirty. He's out on calls.'

'Oh. Well, could you ask him to meet me outside Green Park Underground as soon as he can, it's very urgent.'

'Sure.'

'Thanks very much.'

'You're *more* than welcome.'

I put the phone down. The hag was in the kiosk before I'd got out.

'Who were you callin' – bloody Australia?'

'No, my doctor.' I clutched my forehead. 'I was right . . . I *have* got bubonic plague.'

Her jaw sagged. 'Eh!'

I staggered out of the kiosk, laughing.

CHAPTER THREE

It was just after six when Dennis' Spitfire baaroomed up Piccadilly and swung into the curb. I jumped in and he was off before my pants touched leather.

'Hey, what's up? Sandra said it was urgent.'

I grinned. 'Is that her name? She sounds too much altogether.'

'She is – she's fifty three and weighs eighteen stone.'

'Oh, bollocks . . . another dream shattered.'

He laughed. 'You and every other guy at Zip. But what's the trouble, Russ?'

I heaved a sigh. 'Dennis, you are not going to believe this. You know all that loot I said I have in the bank?'

'Yes.'

'Well, I don't.'

He gaped at me.

I nodded. 'Straight up. Somewhere along the line I miscalculated badly. I waltzed into the bank to cash fifty quid and they waltzed me out again a damn-sight quicker. My account is overdrawn by two pounds forty-two.'

'No!'

'Furthermore, in compliance with Government directives, they couldn't advance me so much as the bus fare to Brompton Road. I had to flog a key-chain to a kid for two pence to make your phone call.'

He still had his mouth open. 'Oh, blimey . . . then . . . the cheque you gave to the hotel . . .'

'Is going to bounce like a Wonderball – and me with it. So, if you don't mind, we'd better go there right now and book me out again.'

'Sure, sure . . . but what are you going to do?'

'Find funds in a hurry. I've been thinking about Zip – do you really think I'd get in?'

'With your experience? Like a shot! Christ, Zebadiah would be chuffed to get you.'

'I haven't got a car, though.'

'Don't worry about it – Zeb will probably lend you one of his vans until you can get something organized. And listen . . . don't worry about somewhere to sleep, I reckon I can get you fixed up at the house, there's an empty room on the top floor. I'll sub you a week's rent.'

'Dennis, that's damn nice of you.'

'Yer . . .' he shrugged, then grinned. 'Now you'll *have* to finish telling me those stories.'

The stiff on the *Excelsior* desk took the news badly.

'You mean . . . you're not even staying *one* night, Mister Tobin?'

'That's right. Something has come up and I have to leave right away.'

'Oh, dear, how unfortunate. But you do realise that we will have to charge you for having occupied the room?'

I frowned. 'But I haven't used it! I mean, I only . . .'

He was shaking his head. 'I'm very sorry, but those are the rules. I must ask you for six pounds fifty for one day's occupancy.'

'But I can't . . .' I was going to tell him I couldn't pay him, but instinct made me hold back. Instead, I gave him a grin and said, 'All right, take it out of the cheque for the thirty I gave you and give me the change.'

He wasn't that green.

'I'm sorry, I can't do that. Under the circumstances I must insist on cash.'

'Cash! I haven't got it and the banks are closed. I'll have to give you a cheque.'

His eyes narrowed. 'Well, all right . . . but remember – we can trace you through your bank if you try to stop payment on it.'

'Now, would I do a thing like that?' I patted my pockets. 'My cheque book's upstairs, I'll give it to you when we come down. Come on, Dennis, let's get packed.'

Up in the room Dennis asked, 'How are you going to get out of this one, Russ?'

'Very fast,' I said, chucking things into the cases. 'Bloody cheek . . . six quid for hanging my clothes up. He's raving mad.'

In five minutes I was all packed. Quickly I wrote out another cheque and we were on our way down to the hall.

'Take the cases out to the car,' I said to Dennis as we crossed the foyer. 'And get ready for a fast getaway.'

'Roger!' he grinned, really enjoying himself.

As he headed out of the door, I approached the desk. 'I'll have that other cheque back, please,' I said pleasantly, waving the new cheque at him.

'Of course. I'm very sorry about having to charge you, sir, but rules are rules.'

'Of course.'

As he brought a cash box from under the counter, I heard the Spitfire roar into life. 'Here you are, sir . . .'

'Thank you. And here's yours.'

While he perused the new cheque, I ripped the old one into umpteen pieces, dropped them into a tin ashtray on the floor, and turned for the door. 'Be seeing you.'

'Thank you, sir . . .'

I was down the steps like a bullet and into the passenger seat with one bound. 'Go!'

Dennis drove the accelerator to the floor. Vaguely, above the screech of tyres, I heard a wail of dismay coming from the doorway of the hotel but didn't turn to acknowledge it. Dennis heard it, too, but didn't ask the question until we were out onto the Brompton Road, heading back to town.

'What was that all about?' he laughed. 'What did you do?'

I shrugged. 'I gave him a cheque for six pounds fifty.'

'So – what was he so mad about?'

'I dunno, it was a perfectly good cheque. Granted, he'll have to wait twenty years to cash it, but it was a perfectly good cheque.'

'You dated it 1997?'

'Did he say otherwise?'

He roared with laughter. 'You know, I reckon you're

going to do all right at Zip Electrics. But first, let's see how you do with the mad Carlotti crowd.'

The house was of a type so familiar to me that, drawing up to it, it was as though the past two years had never happened. A down-at-heel Victorian four-storeys-above-basement, situated in a shabby street of similar abodes, it so resembled Mrs Barnes' boarding house in Liverpool that for an eerie moment, I really believed I was back there.

'Not much,' admitted Dennis as he cut the engine, 'but it's a happy house. If only I could get Ma Carlotti to stop feeding me. Hell, I've got to creep past her door or she yanks me in for a bloody great plate of spaghetti.'

'That can't be bad, Dennis.'

'What – at seven o'clock in the morning!'

'Oh.'

'Tell her you're on a diet or in training or something, otherwise you'll be her size in a month.'

'Big, is she?'

He just laughed.

As we mounted the stone steps to the vestibule, nostalgia swept over me. How long ago it seemed . . . Auntie Barnes, her husband Jack who sat reading the Bible all day and never did a stroke of work, the lovely Jean up there on the top floor, ever-wanton but totally unhaveable – thanks to Auntie's eagle eye . . . how strange I should come back to a house so very like Ravenscourt.

Dennis opened the front door with his key and waved me into a dim, lofty hallway, and immediately my senses were assailed with noise and smell – an aria from 'Rigoletto' in ripping tenor, emanating from upstairs, and the pong of spaghetti and high-powered cheese rolling in from the kitchen.

'Phew!' winced Dennis. 'It's riper than usual, they must have cut into a new one. Hold your nose and follow me.'

We caught the Carlotti family settling down to dinner in the huge old kitchen. Seated round a scrubbed wood table were a middle-aged man and four children, and over at the Aga stove a woman of stupendous girth was ladling out eight tons of spaghetti on to a vast serving plate.

Dennis' appearance at the door triggered off a noisy welcome from the kids, and with a beaming smile Ma Carlotti put down her pan and came towards us.

'Quiet, quiet, mind your manners! Dennis, come eat with us, hey? You bring a friend? Good, he sit down, too, he looks starved.'

Dennis shrugged at me. 'See what I mean? No, thanks, Mrs Carlotti, we've eaten. I'd like you to meet a pal of mine, Russ Tobin. He's just come back from Ireland and he's looking for a room. I was wondering if the room at the top was still vacant?'

'Sure, sure! He can have that one. When you want to move in?'

'Right away, if it's possible,' I said.

'Sure thing. You go look at it, I come up later and make the bed.'

'This is Mr Carlotti,' said Dennis. 'He doesn't speak much English.'

I nodded at dad and got a wave in reply. I got the feeling he didn't speak much of anything with four kids and his wife around.

'And the children,' Dennis continued, 'are Dotty, Spotty, Grotty and Potty Carlotti – Potty's the baby.'

'Hi!' they chorused.

Dotty, a beautiful girl with huge dark eyes, was about eight. Spotty and Grotty, a couple of tearaway lads, looked seven and six respectively, and Potty, another boy, was nudging three. I didn't for a moment believe they were their real names.

'You sure you won't eat?' urged Ma Carlotti. 'I make plenty spaghetti.'

Dennis shook his head and began backing towards the door. 'No, thanks, Mrs C. We'll be going up town later. We'll go up and look at the room.'

We made our exit, Dennis grinning as he led me up the

stairs. 'She's like that all the time – generous to a fault. No one ever starves in this house.'

We clomped up the stairs and reached the first landing, passed several doors, and started up the second flight.

'The Carlottis live on the first floor,' Dennis explained. 'On the second floor there's Bruno, the waiter you met today; Pietro – he's the bloke singing his heart out – he's a cab driver; and myself. On the third floor there's a salesman named Frank Harris – watch out for his practical jokes, he's a nutter; a weirdo layabout named Julian Frost who says he's an actor; and, of course, the delicious and so far mysterious Miss X who's just moved in.'

'Oh, yeh, I'd forgotten about her,' I lied.

'And on the fourth floor there's you!'

'I've got it all to myself?'

'At the moment – yes. There's another room up there, but the Carlottis keep that spare for visiting relatives.'

As we passed along the second landing, Dennis opened the door to his room and I popped my head in. It wasn't a suite at the Savoy but cheerful enough.

'Each floor has its own bathroom,' he explained as we climbed the next flight. 'Except yours. You'll have to use the one on the third floor.'

'That's all right, I'm used to that.'

'Oh?'

'It's incredible. This house is almost identical to the one I lived in in Liverpool. I was on the top floor there, too.'

'Good,' he panted. 'Then you'll be in training for these bloody stairs.'

We reached the third landing. 'That's Frank Harris' room, that's Julian Frost's, that's the bathroom, and that . . .' he grinned, 'is you-know-who's.'

'You should've asked Ma Carlotti what her name is.'

He nodded. 'I'll find out soon enough.' He started up the last flight.

'Bet I find out first,' I grinned.

'How much?'

'A quid.'

'You're on.'

'Right.'

I about-turned, walked back to her door and knocked on it.

'You crafty basket!' he exclaimed, leaning over the banisters. 'That's cheating!'

'It's also winning.'

'No, it isn't.'

'Why?'

He laughed. 'Because she's not in. She works nights – goes out at six and comes in at one in the morning.'

I joined him. 'That sounds interesting. I wonder what she does?'

'The mind boggles.'

We staggered up the last flight and entered my room. It held no surprises.

It was small and had a sloping ceiling to accommodate the pitch of the roof. Its dormer window looked out over our own rear garden and those of the row of similar houses at the back. Well, at least they were gardens, not backyards as had been the case at Ravenscourt.

'What d'you think?' asked Dennis.

'Smashing, mate, I'm very grateful.'

'It's not really. You must have been used to a lot better on your travels.'

'Not at all. This will do very nicely. I'll get moved in right away.'

He was right, of course. I really thought I'd left rooms like this behind me for ever. It was as though I'd made no progress at all in two years. Well, maybe it was a good thing, maybe it would teach me to hang on to my money the next time I had it.

Then, again, maybe it wouldn't. What the hell, you can only spend it once, and I wouldn't have swapped the past two years for anything.

By eight o'clock I was settled in. Mrs Carlotti had made the bed, and had given me a bedside lamp which made the room more cosy. I can't stand ceiling lights.

'Better,' nodded Dennis, inspecting the finished product. 'Yeh, not bad at all. I reckon we ought to christen it.'

'How?'

'I'll be back in a minute.'

He returned with a bottle of Scotch, two glasses and a pitcher of water. 'I've had this since I moved in, I've been waiting for someone to drink it with. To be honest, I did have someone of the opposite sex in mind, but if I wait for that to happen the damn stuff will evaporate.'

'How about the scrumptuous Miss X?'

'Yes, well . . . working the hours she does, I'll be lucky if I ever *see* her again, never mind anything else. Maybe she takes a day off on Sunday.'

He poured a couple of hefties, and added a gesture of water. 'Cheers, Russ.'

'Cheers, old son, and thanks again. I won't forget this.'

'Nah . . .'

He sat down in the cane chair by the bed and I sat on the bed, propped against the wooden headboard. He got his fags out and offered me one.

'I can't even give you a cigarette,' I said. 'Jesus, this being broke business is terrible!'

'Never mind, you'll soon be back on top. I reckon a week with Zip and you'll be moving out of here and into the Carlton Tower.'

I laughed. 'Dennis, your faith in me is quite touching.'

'What – with your experience? You'll be earning a hundred a week straight off, I'll bet you. Hell, if a dumb bugger like me can earn seventy and eighty . . .'

I whistled. 'You do that well, hm?'

'Sure. All you've got to do is put in the number of calls, Russ, and Zeb will keep you supplied with plenty of leads.'

I nodded. 'Well, it certainly sounds like the answer to my problem. What d'you think I ought to do about it?'

He shrugged. 'Come to work with me tomorrow morning. They *are* advertising for more men, Zeb will be delighted to see you.'

'Okay, fine. What time do we leave?'

'Eight o'clock. Breakfast is at seven-thirty in the dining-room.'

He grinned. 'You'll meet the inmates then.'

'Fine.'

He took another gulp of Scotch. 'Okay, so let's hear it.'

'Hm? What?'

'The male escort job you did in Australia.'

'Aw, Dennis . . .'

'Now, now! I shall cut off your fag supply!'

'That's dirty!'

'Yeh, I'll bet the story is, too. Carry on, Russell.'

I finally poured him out of my room around midnight, and only managed to get rid of him then because the Scotch was all gone.

'Nightie night, Russell!' he warbled, falling down the last three stairs. 'Don' be late f'breakfast!'

'Sssshh! G'night, Dennis.'

I closed the door, fell across the bed and lay there watching the ceiling change places with the floor. What is this life if, full of care, we have no time to lie and stare . . . No, this certainly wasn't my room at Ravenscourt. The cracks on the ceiling there resembled Jesus standing in a bucket . . . and these cracks looked more like Danny La Rue water-skiing.

Round and round he went . . . round and round and . . .

He was still at it when my alarm clock went off at seven.

CHAPTER FOUR

Ugh! And as soon as I entered the dining-room I could tell Dennis was feeling the same.

I entered diffidently, a stranger to the club. At the long dining table in the dowdy room sat Bruno, the waiter I'd already met, Dennis and three other men. There was a young, dark, handsome lad – presumably Pietro, the singing cab driver; a small, chubby, cheerful-looking salesman, Frank Harris; and a pale, aesthetic-looking creature with an abundance of dark wiry, unkempt hair that resembled an exploded sofa. Julian Frost, no doubt.

Frank Harris started his nonsense as soon as I appeared. 'I spy strangers!' he called. 'Stranger in the house!'

I winced at the noise. 'Good morning . . . I'm Russ Tobin.'

'Oh, we've heard all about you,' said Harris. 'Shame on you, leading our poor innocent Dennis astray like that. Just look at him, he looks like somethin' the cat dragged in. Shame . . . are you feeling poorly, then, Den? What you need is a hair of the dog. Tobin, nip into the kitchen and pull a hair out of Fido, will you, ha ha ha . . . don't mind me, I'm always this repulsive.' He held out his hand. 'Frank Harris is the name . . . I'm in ladies' dresses. It's not my fault, my mother wanted a daughter . . . ha ha ha.'

I took his hand. Zzzziiippp! an electric shock ripped up my arm.

'CHRIST!'

'Ha ha ha, just my little joke,' he chortled, pocketing the gadget.

'Oh, for God*sake*, Harris . . .' tutted Frost. 'Can't we have *one* breakfast without your puerile practical jokes, I mean really!'

'Now, don't get your knickers in a twist, Julian, dear, this place'd be a morgue without me. Sit there, Tobin, next to Dennis, you can keep him from falling asleep in his porridge.'

I pulled out the chair and sat down. I should have known better. The concealed whoopee cushion let go a resounding raspberry that shook the room.

Harris almost fell out of his chair laughing. 'Oh, Tobin, you dirty devil . . .'

'For God*sake*!' exclaimed Julian.

'Silly bastard,' muttered Dennis.

At that moment Mrs Carlotti entered, bearing a huge server of bacon and eggs. 'Good morning, good morning, good morning . . . here you are, boys, eat hearty, there's plenty for everyone. You want some more, you ask.'

She placed the plate in the centre of the table. 'Now you have everything . . . toast, tea, coffee? Good. Eat up, you can't do good work on empty stomach.'

As she left the room, Harris made a dive for the plate, scraped two eggs and three rashers of bacon on his own plate and began attacking it with sickening gusto.

More genteelly, Bruno, Pietro and Julian helped themselves and began their meal. Gingerly, I picked up my plate and made a move to do the same, but suddenly the sight of all those running eggs and greasy bacon was too much for my delicate disposition.

'I, er . . .' I turned to Dennis. 'Somehow, I . . .'

Eyes bulging and green-gilled, he nodded frantically and shot to his feet.

'Excuse us, gentlemen!' I said, hurrying for the door.

'Ha ha ha!' chuckled Frank Harris. 'Well, all the more for us, lads!'

We ran along the hall and burst out of the front door into the cool morning air, and there, by Dennis' car, we stood and gulped down great lungfuls of the stuff.

'Phew, that's better,' gasped Dennis, looking a touch more human. 'It wasn't the food so much as that silly bugger Harris. His jokes really make me sick.'

'Anybody ever get back at him, Dennis?'

His eyes crinkled. 'No . . . but I've got a feeling somebody's going to.'

'Let's give it some thought, hm?'

'You're on. Come on, there's a little caff near Zip, we can have a quiet cup of coffee and plan Harris' destruction.'

At eight-thirty sharp we entered the premises of Zip Electrics. At first sight it was anything but impressive, merely a small shopfront, newly-painted white, with a window crammed with electrical goods – vacuum cleaners, radios, sewing machines, toasters, you name it. And the shop itself was equally unstartling, just an ordinary little elecrical shop with a few display stands and a glass counter.

Behind the counter was a desk and at the desk sat a stout, middle-aged woman with fading red hair. The silken-voiced Sandra, I presumed – the unwary salesman's Siren.

'Morning, Sandra,' said Dennis, walking behind the counter. 'I've brought a new recruit along. You've already spoken to him . . . this is Russ Tobin.'

'Ah, yes! I didn't know you were looking for a job when I spoke to you.'

'I didn't know either. Dennis convinced me I ought to quit the chairmanship of Shell and join Zip Electrics – so here I am.'

'Russ has had experience selling sewing machines in Liverpool,' said Dennis. 'This is a natural for him.'

'Wonderful!' said Sandra. 'Mr Polkoski will be pleased. We've got three other new ones in this morning, but they've had no previous selling experience. I'll let him know you're here.'

She disappeared through a door at the rear of the shop.

'The warehouse and offices are at the back,' explained Dennis. 'Don't be fooled by the size of the shop, this is just the tip of the iceberg. Well, I'd better get cracking, Russ, I've got nine calls today and I've got to load my appliances. Best of luck, I'll see you back at the house, hm?'

'Fine, Dennis. Sell a million, we need the money.'

'Roger.'

As he went through the door, Sandra Keane returned. 'Come on through, Russ. Mr Polkoski is just about to start training the new men, so you can join them.'

'How long does the training last?' I asked.

'All day. He makes sure his men are confident before he lets them out on the road.'

'Oh. I was hoping to start selling today.'

'My, you're keen,' she laughed. 'Well, maybe with your experience you won't need so much training. Anyway, see how it goes.'

The warehouse we had entered was enormous, as big as an aircraft hangar. Over on the right, cartoned appliances were stacked almost to the roof. To the left ran a line of glass-fronted offices in which several girls were working. Sandra led me towards one of these.

We passed through the office into a room beyond. Here, three young men were seated in wooden chairs before a small raised stage on which the Zip appliances were displayed on pedestals. Also on the stage was a kitchen table and a couple of chairs, their purpose familiar to me.

'Take a seat, Russ,' said Sandra. 'Mr Polkoski will be with you in a moment.'

As I sat down, she went back through the office.

I nodded to the three lads. Two of them looked decent enough and suitably nervous; the third, however, a red-headed gink in a loud suit with a mouth to match, looked like trouble.

'Yers, it's plain as day . . .' he said to the others, as though continuing an interrupted conversation, 'it's all bin knocked orf, take my word. Fell orf the back of a lorry, know what I mean? Stands to reason you can't flog stuff at these prices and be legit, nar can you? Don't make sense.'

'Perhaps he works on small profits and big turn-over?' suggested one chap in a brown suit. 'I don't think it's right to accuse the man of illegitimate dealing before he's had a chance to explain his method of selling.'

'Oh, hoity-toity,' mocked Red Head. 'Lissen, I've bin around, mate, I can smell a knock-orf at four 'undred yards.'

'Yes, no doubt,' drolled Brown Suit.

Red was about to reply, but the door opened and a small, middle-aged, pear-shaped man in crumpled grey slacks and a wilted white shirt came through, carrying a clip-board. He came towards us, and regarded us one by one over the rim of his glasses, then stepped up on the dais.

'Good morning, gentlemen, thank you for coming. My name is Polkoski . . . Zebadiah Isaac Polkoski – which might give you some idea why my company is called Zip Electrics. I am going to tell you about our appliances . . . what we sell and how we sell them. If, when I have finished, any of you feel that this method of selling is not for you, I would be obliged if you would simply walk out. I would not wish to waste any more of your precious time. I am interested only in men who can sell our products with a good heart. All right?' He nodded. 'All right . . .'

He turned and gestured to the appliances on display. 'Here is our line . . . twenty different appliances, all of manageable size. But . . .' he let the word hang, ensuring our attention, '. . . in each case there is a *cheap* model, called the Mark One, and an *expensive* model, known as the Super De Luxe . . . Remember that.

'Now, here,' from the clipboard he released a double page from a newspaper, opened it out and held it up. It was a huge Zip Appliances ad. proclaiming bargains at suicidal prices. 'This is the kind of advertising we do . . . and this is how you get your leads. You don't have to go knocking on doors, the customer comes to *you*. Here, at the bottom of the page, is a coupon. The customer fills in this coupon requesting a demonstration of the appliance, so when you arrive at the house you are *welcomed in*, you don't have to fight your way in.

'Now . . . in most cases, because the Mark One appliance is such excellent value, you will quickly make a sale. But this is *not* the sale you are after. There is no money in it for anyone – not for you and not for me, which is why I can afford to pay you only *two percent* on such a sale. No – the sale you are after is the Super De Luxe appliance which you will bring in and demonstrate *after* you have sold the Mark One, understand?'

We all nodded that we understood.

To me it was old hat. It was precisely the way Ritebuy had sold their sewing machines. And I must admit I couldn't help feeling a bit superior sitting there, a slight tendency to smother a yawn. This really was teaching your granny to suck eggs.

'During that demonstration,' Polkoski continued, 'you point out how much better *value* the Super De Luxe model is . . . it's better *quality,* longer *guarantee period, better* supply of *spare parts,* etcetera, etcetera, and if you've done a good job selling . . .' he shrugged, 'you've got a sale. And you've earned yourself *ten* percent of the higher price. Believe me, gentlemen, it works.'

Polkoski allowed this bit of inspiring propaganda to sink in, then, in a let's-get-down-to-business tone of voice, continued. Unclipping a pamphlet from the board he held it aloft, pausing dramatically for a moment to allow its importance to overwhelm us.

'This . . . is your Bible – the Zip training manual. It contains the salient selling features of all our appliances, one double-page being devoted to each appliance.' He opened the pamphlet and exhibited a speciment double-page.

'Here, on the left-hand page, are the details of the cheap Mark One appliance. And here, on the right-hand page, are the details of the more expensive Super De Luxe model. You will read, mark, learn and inwardly digest *all* these facts until you know them better than you know your own names. That is the only way to sell successfully. Understand?'

We gave another nod.

'Right . . .' From the clip-board he produced three 'bibles' and held them out to Red Head. 'Distribute these, please . . . and turn to page one, gentlemen.'

While we were turning, Polkoski crossed to one of the pedestal stands and brought a food mixer back to the table, connecting its plug to an electrical outlet set in the top of the table.

'You . . .' he said, pointing to Brown Suit. 'Read out the selling points of this Food Mixer Mark One, please . . . slowly.'

The lad cleared his throat. 'The Zip Mixer Mark One has an attractive, washable, plastic casing . . .' 'An attractive, washable, plastic casing . . .' repeated Polkoski, pointing to the appropriate part of the machine.

'A powerful, three-speed, 240-watt motor . . .'

'A powerful, three-speed, 240-watt motor,' intoned Polkoski.

'Unique double-beater action . . . unbreakable, hygienic plastic mixing bowl . . . replacement whisk . . . and indispensable dough hook.'

'Right,' nodded Polkoski. 'And what more could a housewife expect for a mere twenty-two pounds fifty? Believe me, gentlemen, there is no better food-mixer value on the market today than the Zip Mark One. All right, so let us suppose . . .' he looked round the group and stabbed a finger at me, 'you. Tobin, isn't it? You've sold sewing machines?'

'Yes, I have.'

'Good, then you've probably done this before. Come up on the stage and play the part of the housewife.'

To the others he explained, 'Mrs Tobin here has sent in a coupon requesting a demonstration of the Zip Food Mixer Mark One. I shall be the salesman.' He waved me into one of the chairs at the table, then rapped on the table, 'Good morning, Mrs Tobin. I am Zebadiah Polkoski of Zip Electrics. You sent in a coupon asking for a demonstration of the Zip Food Mixer Mark One? May I come in? Thank you.'

He turned to the audience. 'One *vital* point to remember – always, *always* insist on a table large enough to contain the *two* appliances side-by-side. In this way a constant comparison between the two can be maintained by the housewife. A new Austin Mini car may look most appealing by itself, but when you put it beside a brand new Rolls Royce . . .' He shrugged, 'Need I say more? All right, so we have our housewife comfortably settled in her kitchen and we unpack the Food Mixer Mark One. There, Mrs Tobin, do you not agree it's a handsome appliance?'

'Beautiful,' I agreed.

'Just look at its attractive, washable, plastic casing . . . how well it complements your magnificent kitchen. Now we plug it in and switch on. There . . . note the powerful, three-speed, 240-watt motor – a triumph of electrical engineering. Note the unique double-beater action, what glorious cakes you will make with this machine . . .'

It took Polkoski only a few minutes to dem. the egg whisk and the pastry hook, then he came in for the fast close.

'At a mere twenty-two pounds fifty, Mrs Tobin, you have the finest food-mixer value on the market today . . . and how did you wish to pay for it – cash or cheque?'

'Er . . . cheque.'

'Splendid. I can leave this machine with you right now and you can begin making those wonderful cakes right away.'

He turned to the audience. 'All right, in nine cases out of ten you will make the sale of the Mark One that easily. You take the cheque, make out the receipt, and *then* you ask: Mrs Tobin, did you happen to hear our advertisement on commercial radio this week?'

I looked suitably blank. 'No.'

'You didn't! Mrs Tobin, please excuse me for a moment, I'll be right back.' He moved away, towards the Zip Food Mixer Super De Luxe, explaining to us, 'Now, this is where you return to your car and bring in the magnificent Super De Luxe model. Returning to the house, you place the De Luxe right beside the Mark One . . . and as you can see, the difference in quality is immediately apparent.'

As he placed the Super De Luxe on the table, I went into the act I'd learned so well at Ritebuy.

'Oh, my word, that's fantastic, Mr Polkoski, but it looks *terribly* expensive.'

He grinned at me. 'Yes, you've sold sewing machines before.' Now he became the salesman again. 'This, Mrs Tobin, is our exciting new Super De Luxe model. Of course, it *is* more expensive than the Mark One, but then you'd expect it to be, wouldn't you?'

'Oh, I couldn't afford anything like that, Mr Polkoski.'

'Mrs Tobin – relax, I'm not trying to sell it to you. Why should I, you've just bought a mixer! No, I'm paid to *demonstrate* it to you, then you can tell all your friends about it. I'll only take a few minutes of your time. The first thing you will notice about the Super De Luxe is, of course, that it belongs in a very different class to the Mark One. Oh, please don't misunderstand me, the Mark One is a very fine machine! Just as a Mini is a very fine car – in its own class! But of course, compared with a Rolls Royce . . .'

'Yes, of course,' I admitted, glancing askance at the Mark One I'd just bought. 'And what precisely does the Super De Luxe do that my Mark One won't do?'

He spread his hands. 'Let me show you.'

Polkoski did a fine dem. and by the time he'd finished singing the praises of the slow-speed outlet, the mincer, the slicer and shredder, the can-opener, the coffee grinder, the juice extractor, the potato peeler and the liquidizer, he almost had *me* convinced the Super De Luxe was worth the staggering price of one hundred and thirty pounds.

'It's beautiful . . . beautiful,' I sighed, 'but how could I ever afford it?'

'Ah, ha!' he pounced, waving my imaginary cheque at me. 'Well, now, it just so happens, Mrs Tobin, that what you have paid me for the Mark One is precisely the amount required as a down-payment on the Super . . . and you could pay off the balance on HP payments over two years, if you wish. Now, let's see what that would work out at . . .'

He turned to the audience with a victorious shrug. 'There it is, gentlemen, that is how to sell Zip appliances.

Believe me – it works! Provided you learn the selling points of each appliance *by heart* so that you can dem. each of them with great confidence, your success rate will be very high indeed – and so will your earnings. All right, now you know our method of selling. If it appeals to you, please remain seated . . . if it doesn't, you are free to leave right now.'

Nobody moved.

He nodded. 'Good. No doubt you will have some questions to ask at this point?'

Red Head stuck his hand up. 'How do we get paid?'

'You are paid on firm sales at the end of each week.'

'Do we get any petrol allowance?'

Polkoski shook his head and again held up the double-page advertisement. 'This sort of advertising, which will provide you with all the leads you can handle, is extremely expensive. I can't afford to pay you a penny more than the commissions I've already outlined.'

Red Head asked, 'What about trade-ins?'

Polkoski again shook his head. 'We cannot accept trade-ins, they're too much trouble.'

'So what happens if the old dear is crackers about the Super vacuum cleaner but needs to get rid of her old one?'

Polkoski shrugged. 'She sells it privately . . . gives it away to a friend.'

Red Head grinned. 'Could *we* do a little deal on the side, then?'

Polkoski's eyed narrowed suspiciously. 'Any arrangement you care to make regarding a trade-in is purely a private affair between yourself and the customer and has *nothing* to do with Zip. Zip will bear no responsibility whatever for any such transaction . . . and this is clearly stated on the back of our receipt forms. Be warned, however, that if such a transaction is conducted in either an unjust or illegal manner and results in any form of trouble with the law, you are on your own and will lose your job with Zip instantly. Is that quite clear?'

'Sure,' grinned Red Head.

I had a feeling he wasn't going to last very long.

'Any further questions?' asked Polkoski.

'Yes,' said Brown Suit. 'How are the leads distributed?'

'At my sole discretion,' Polkoski answered firmly. 'I will be as fair as I can, but I will not waste expensive leads on a man who cannot make the best use of them. Any more questions?'

There were none.

'Good,' nodded Polkoski. 'We will now go through the appliances one by one.' He turned to me with a smile. 'Are you ready, Mrs Tobin?'

'Ready.'

'This will make you feel at home. We come now to the Zip sewing machine Mark One . . .'

We spent all morning on the appliances, breaking at eleven o'clock for a quick coffee, then we were back at it again until lunch at one o'clock. By then I'd had enough. I wanted to start selling.

Red Head and the other two adjourned to a local pub for a pint and a sandwich, but I didn't go with them. Instead, I popped into a near-by coffee shop, had a quick bite with a fiver Dennis had lent me, and got back ten minutes early to beard Polkoski before the afternoon session. When I arrived he was in his office, eating a sandwich and perusing a girlie magazine which he slid into a drawer before beckoning me in. I entered.

'Sorry to disturb your lunch, Mr Polkoski, but I wondered if I could have a word with you before we start again?'

'Sure, come in, sit down. You did a good job for me this morning, I appreciate it. How long were you on sewing machines?'

'About a year. It was for Ritebuy . . . in Liverpool.'

'Were you successful?'

I grinned modestly. 'Pretty good. That's what I came to see you about. I . . . really feel I've got the hang of your system now, and I wondered if I could get cracking this afternoon? Frankly, I need the money pretty badly.'

He grinned. 'That's what I like to hear. There's no

salesman like a hungry salesman. Sandra tells me you haven't got a car yet.'

'That's right. She said maybe we could come to some arrangement about the loan of one of your vans?'

He nodded. 'Ordinarily it's something I wouldn't even consider for a new man, but in your case . . .' He had a think about it, then nodded again. 'All right, Tobin, let's see what you're made of.' He opened a folder and took out three clipped coupons. 'I'll lend you a van for this afternoon and you can follow up these three leads . . . an electric kettle, a food mixer and a vacuum cleaner. If you're successful, we'll work something out about the van until you can get a car of your own. Now,' he got up and went to a filing cabinet standing against the wall, 'you'll need a Zip bible . . . a receipt book . . . and a pad of HP forms – make sure they are filled out correctly.'

He moved back to his desk, put the items in a cardboard folder and handed it to me.

'Go over to Goods Outward on the other side of the warehouse, show the storeman, Ted Faulter, your three leads and he will give you your six appliances. In the meantime I will arrange to have a van made available to you.'

'Thank you very much, Mr Polkoski, I appreciate it.'

'Show me how much by selling three Super appliances,' he smiled. 'Remember, those leads cost me five pounds each, treat them as though they were five pound notes.'

'I will. And thanks again.'

I left his office floating on air. Boy, it was good to be back in action – and back in the money. I'd show Polkoski how to sell. He'd need a bigger warehouse by the end of the week.

I crossed to the Goods Outward Department, went through a door and entered a small reception area which had a counter, the flap of which was raised, giving access to the store area beyond.

I looked around, knocked on the counter, called out, 'Anybody here?' but got no response. The place was deserted.

I ventured beyond the counter, wandered right into the stores area, looking left and right, and was half-way down a row of cartoned appliances when suddenly a voice behind me barked, ' 'ey! What the 'ell d'you think you're doing in 'ere?'

I spun round, heart thumping. He was a weasely little bloke in a brown overall, with a mouth like a razor slash.

'Er . . . Mister Faulter?'

'Who the 'ell are you? Come on, get out of my stores!'

'I'm Russ Tobin. I . . .'

'Out!'

'I . . . came for . . .'

He strode up to me and clamped a bony hand on my arm. 'Don't care what you came for, mate, just get the 'ell out of my *stores*!'

Anger erupted inside me. This was Ritebuy all over again, only there the little rat's name was O'Neill and he was our Sales Manager. He'd made my life hell for almost a year and I wasn't going to put up with that again.

I looked down at the hand on my arm. 'Take that off, Faulter, or *I'll* take it off.'

'Ho, will you, now!' he retorted, giving me a shove towards the counter. 'Go on – out . . . Out! Get behind that counter!'

I gaped at him. 'Who the hell d'you think you are, you pushy little bastard?'

'I'm the Stores Superintendent, that's who! And can't you bleedin' read?' He flung an arm at a notice on the reception wall. 'No unauthorized entry into Stores Area! That means you!'

I waved the three coupons under his nose. 'This is my authority – I want appliances! I'm a new salesman!'

'I don't care a monkey's if you're the fucking Pope – you don't set foot in my warehouse without my permission! Now, if you want those appliances, get behind the counter!'

Fuming, I sauntered back through the flap which he closed with a crash. 'Now . . . what d'you want?'

I slammed the coupons down on the counter. Peevishly

he snatched them up and ambled off, muttering under his breath.

Bloody marvellous, I thought, shaking with anger. There always had to be one miserable sod in any organization, one jumped-up, power-drunk little squirt to make life miserable. Well, this one wasn't going to get away with it. If I had any more trouble with Ted Bloody Faulter I'd feed him through a sewing machine and stitch his mouth shut.

There was a lot of crashing and banging about among the appliances, then up he came with my stuff on a trolley. Lifting the flap, he shoved the trolley through to me, then lowered the flap again.

'Sign here . . . and make sure you bring the trolley back or next time you won't get one.'

'Tell me something, Faulter,' I said, wiping a signature across a receipt, 'have you tried All Bran? I hear it works wonders for a constipated disposition.'

'Don't you talk to me like that, you cheeky young bugger! Go on, get out of here!'

Grabbing up the receipt, he stormed off round a bank of appliances. I pushed the trolley out into the warehouse, encountering a pimple-faced youth who was also wearing a brown overall, on which the name-tape said he was Alan.

'You Mister Tobin?'

'Yes.'

'I've got a van for you . . . out in the yard.'

'Thank you, would you show me the way, Alan?' As we walked, I asked him, 'Is Ted Faulter always vile tempered?'

'Bin havin' a go at you, has he? What did you do – set foot in his stores?'

'Yes, but you'd think I'd broken into his house and raped his daughter, the way he went on.'

'Silly old cunt. Yeh, he's always like that, thinks he owns the bleedin' place. Be careful of him he can be a nasty little bastard if he gets his knife into you. No telling what he'll do.'

We went out into a yard and crossed it to one of three little Ford vans lined up in a row.

'I've given you the best of them,' he said, 'which ain't saying much, but it'll do you for a while. Sign here, please. Keys are inside and there's plenty of petrol.'

'Do I have to bring it back tonight – or can I take it home?'

'You can take it to the pictures for all I care,' he grinned, turning away. 'Happy selling.'

'You bet.'

I loaded the boxed appliances into the back of the van, then climbed into the driving seat and studied the three leads. The kettle was for a Mrs Hennessey of Flat 12, 804 Redcliffe Gardens, the vacuum cleaner for a Mrs Diamond on Wimbledon Park Side, and the food mixer for a Mrs Barry of 226 Paradise Road, Bermondsey. In the glove-compartment of the van I found a dog-eared A.1. Atlas of London, and spent a few minutes planning my route, finally deciding to do Mrs Hennessey first, Mrs Barry second, then Mrs Diamond in Wimbledon last, being closest to home.

I started the engine but for a moment longer sat there and really brought my mind to bear on what I was about to do. I was going out to sell three Super De Luxe appliances . . . to *sell* three *Super De Luxe* appliances – not simply to knock on the door and deliver three Mark Ones. It had to be three out of three, nothing less. Tomorrow morning I had to report to Polkoski one hundred percent success, nothing less. It had to be total victory – because, hell, all other considerations aside, I needed the money!'

Thus inspired and internally fired, I set my sights on Flat 12, 804 Redcliffe Gardens and fed Mrs Hennessey into my Sales Resistance Annihilation Computer.

Blip! I pressed the button. There was now no way she could escape. May as well give up right now, love, the Zip Electric Super De Luxe kettle is as good as yours!

And with a carefree, cavalier laugh I let out the clutch and drove out of the yard, heading towards the Fulham Road – and to victory!

CHAPTER FIVE

Some fifteen minutes later, I drew up at number 804 Redcliffe Gardens – a tall Georgian terraced town house rising four storeys above the pavement. I cut the engine and opened my folder, took out the Zip training manual and once again went over the various selling points, though to be sure there wasn't much to learn about the Zip kettle. The difference between the Mark One and the Super De Luxe was self-evident quality, though the Super did have an automatic cut-out which operated when the kettle boiled.

Right – I was ready. I got out of the van, took the Mark One out of the back, climbed several stone steps to the vestibule and pressed the button for Flat 12.

The speaker grille crackled. 'Yes, who is it?'

'Mrs Hennessey?'

'Yes?'

'Zip Electric, Mrs Hennessey. I've brought your kettle.'

'Oh! All right, come on up.'

The front door buzzed. I pushed it open and entered a dismal hallway, closing the door behind me.

'Up here!' called a voice above me.

I looked up . . . and up . . . and up . . . discovering a pin-sized head leaning over the banisters at around thirty thousand feet.

Oh, rotten hell . . .

'Is there a lift, Mrs Hennessey?' I shouted up.

'I'm afraid not! You'll have to do it the hard way!'

Yes, I'd forgotten – the Mrs Hennesseys of the world always live on the top floor. Still, it could have been worse – she might have ordered a forty-pound sewing machine.

Clump . . . clump . . . clump . . . up I went. Round and round and up and up . . . finally arriving at the top floor, stupendously knackered.

She was waiting in her doorway, a nice old soul with grey hair and glasses, looked like a retired schoolteacher. She smiled sympathetically, unveiling huge tomb-stone teeth. 'Awful stairs, aren't they? I only go out once a week, I simply can't face them. Do come in, Mr . . .?'

'Tobin,' I gasped. 'Russ Tobin.'

I followed her into the kitchen that smelled like the Battersea Dogs' Home. No wonder – there were three of them, three snuffling Pekinese, in a basket in the middle of the floor, though not for long. As I entered, they launched a concerted attack at me, filling the kitchen with ear-splitting yaps until driven back by their mistress.

'Frou Frou . . . Mitzi . . . Charles . . . Be quiet! Be quiet!'

Snuffling and sneezing, they reluctantly retreated into the basket and shut up. Silence reigned, though not for long. From behind me came a piercing shriek that made me jump . . . followed by a raucous squawk, and I turned to find a mynah bird in one cage and a big grey parrot in another. In yet another cage were nine million budgies and now, excited by all the barking and shrieking and squawking, these started up, which got the mynah bird and the parrot going once more, which started the bleeding dogs off again.

The place was a madhouse!

'Quiet . . . quiet, all of you!' commanded Mrs Hennessey, and not one of them took a blind bit of notice of her. She turned to me, smiling. 'It's the hot weather, you know, it makes them a bit fretful.' Her eyes went to the cartoned kettle. 'May I see it?'

'But of course!' I said, putting the box down on the table and folding back the flaps. 'This is the one you sent for, Mrs Hennessey, the Zip Electric Kettle Mark One . . . I'd like to demonstrate it for you. May I fill it?'

'Of course.'

Cautiously skirting the dog basket, I crossed to the sink, filled the kettle and came back to the table. 'Now, we'll just plug it in and you'll see . . . how . . . wonderfully fast . . .'

I stared down into the carton. There was no bloody flex in there! They'd forgotten to pack the lead!

'Anything the matter?' asked Mrs Hennessey.

'Er . . .' I laughed. 'A slight hitch, I'm afraid, I , er . . . left the lead in the car, Mrs Hennessey, I'll have to go down for it.'

'Oh, dear . . . you'll have to climb all those stairs again.'

'My own fault,' I said lightly. 'Won't be a tick.'

I thumped down the stairs, cursing Ted Faulter. He'd done this on purpose, I knew. All the cartons had been opened, as they should have been if the appliances had been checked in the stores, and he'd taken the goddam lead out!

I'd kill him! I wouldn't sew his lips together, I'd stitch the end of his dick up, then force a gallon of water down his throat and laugh while he burst all over the warehouse.

At the van I opened the carton containing the Super De Luxe kettle and was relieved to find it did have a lead. It did *not*, however, have a plug on the end! Oh, fine start, this was. I'd have to stuff the loose wires into the wall! Very impressive dem., I must say.

I threw the lead back into the carton and took the carton out of the van. I was buggered if I'd come all the way down again for the Super kettle. I'd leave it outside the door of her apartment until I did the switch.

I locked up the van and headed back up the steps, pushed on the front door and nearly broke my wrist. It was locked again! Muttering dark oaths, I pressed her button.

'Yes?'

'Mrs Hennessey, I've locked myself out!'

'Oh dear.'

The front door buzzed and I went through, and five days later I staggered up the last flight of stairs, legs like jelly.

Damn, she was waiting at the door for me!

'Oh, what's that you've got – another kettle?'

'I, er . . . well, yes, its . . . its lead will fit yours, Mrs Hennessey.'

She frowned, obviously puzzled as to why I'd carried the

kettle up the stairs instead of just the lead, but didn't say anything.

Again I followed her into the flat and got another tumultuous welcome from the menagerie, and this time one of the Pekes peed on my foot.

'Charles, you *naughty* boy, how dare you do that to a guest!' admonished Mrs H.

'It's . . . quite all right,' I said, shaking my shoe. 'I hear it's an old Chinese custom.'

'Get back in your basket, you dirty dog! Just for that you'll get no tea.'

Charlie's expression said he didn't give a stuff, it had been worth it.

I took the lead out of the Super box, plugged it in the Mark One kettle, stuck my pen into the wall socket to open the safety gates, and fed the loose red and black wires into it.

'Sorry I have to do this, Mrs Hennessey, but they didn't put a plug on the lead.'

'Dear me,' she tutted, 'they don't seem terribly efficient at Zip Electrics, do they? I'm not sure I like this at all. Who exactly *are* they, Mr Tobin?'

'Zip Electrics? Well, they . . .' I gave a shrug. 'Well, they're a company, Mrs Hennessey.'

'Are they long established?'

'Er, yes, I think so.'

'You don't sound too sure,' she said suspiciously. 'How long have you worked for them?'

Oh, Gawd . . .

'Well, to tell you the truth, I . . . I only started today.'

Her face fell. 'I see.' She looked closely at the Mark One, her nose wrinkling with suspicion and disdain. 'Mm . . . can't say I'm over-impressed with it, Mr Tobin . . . I've seen better for six pounds twenty. The finish seems rather poor to me. Where was it made?'

'Er . . . I believe it's a product of the British Empire, Mrs Hennessey, but it's remarkably good value and fully guaran . . .'

'You mean Hong Kong? Oh, dear, I wish I'd known,

I wouldn't *dream* of buying anything made in Hong Kong.'

'Yes, well . . .'

She put her hand on the kettle. 'Are you sure it's switched on? Nothing seems to be happening.'

'Oh? Oh. Well . . . perhaps I haven't put the wires in properly . . .'

With fast-fading heart I wiggled the wires around in the socket, knowing the sale was already dead. In any sale, if you get off to a bad start like this you have to work ten times harder to make up lost ground and hardly ever make it.

Well, I thought, nothing ventured. I decided to go straight in with the Super De Luxe.

'Mrs Hennessey, I can see you're not very impressed with this kettle, so I'm going to show you something else. I have here the Zip Super De Luxe kettle, a *far* superior appliance for only a few pounds more . . .'

I pulled out the Super and plonked it down next to the Mark One.

'Oh!' she said, her eyes lighting up. 'Oh, that does look better.'

'It most certainly is better. Better all-round quality – *plus* the added advantage of this automatic button which switches off the kettle when it boils. Let me show you how it works . . .'

'Er . . . how much is it, Mr Tobin?'

I shrugged. 'A mere twelve pounds forty – and there isn't another kettle on the market to touch it at that price.'

She gasped and clutched her bosom. 'Twelve pounds forty! Good heavens, I couldn't afford that!'

I smiled understandingly. 'Now, never you mind about that, we'll work something out. First let me show you how it works . . .'

'No, no, I *know* how it works Mr Tobin – it boils water is how it works. Now, please, *no* . . . put it back in its box, I can't afford it. Besides, on second thoughts, I really think I prefer to buy a kettle from Harrods or Barkers.'

'Oh, come, Mrs Hennessey, there's no need to doubt Zip Appliances, they *are* fully guaranteed . . .'

'Yes, yes, I'm sure, but . . . no, I don't want it,' she insisted, holding up her hands as though to defend herself against the beastly thing. 'Now, please . . . put it in its box.'

She was getting frightened, I could see the signs, and no salesman *ever* sold anything to a panicked customer. I gave her a relaxed smile and a comforting shrug.

'All right, Mrs Hennessey, as you wish . . . but I would just like to fill it and show you how the automatic button works . . .'

She made with the hands again and darted looks to left and right as though searching for an avenue of escape. 'Please, Mr Tobin, no! I . . . I don't like the sound of Zip Electrics. It sounds fly-by-night.'

'Fly-by-night! Mrs Hennessey, I assure you . . .'

'*How* can you assure me, Mister Tobin, this is your first day with them. Now, *please* . . . pack up your kettles and leave!'

'Mrs Hennessey, believe me, I . . .'

'No!' she shouted, getting quite hysterical, the panic in her voice starting the bloody dogs off again. 'Please GO! . . . or I shall call the police!'

Oh, my God . . .

'All right, all right, I'm going! Just . . . calm down, Mrs Hennessey . . .'

I wrenched the wires out of the wall socket, shoved the Mark One back in its box, put the Super box on top of it and picked up both cartons – forgetting the Mark One was still full of water. Yerk . . . out it shot, all down the front of my trousers.

Mrs H. raced for the front door and flung it open, stood there white-faced as I hobbled past her, water running into my shoes.

'Mrs Hennessey, I assure you . . .'

Bang! The door closed in my face.

Ted Faulter, I seethed as I squelched down the stairs, your hour has come. Just wait till I get back! I shall feed your balls into a food-mixer whisk and turn it up to full power . . . I shall stuff the upholstery tube of a Zip vacuum cleaner up your arse and suck your eyeballs out of their sockets! Ooh, I was livid.

I threw the mucking kettles into the back of the can, emptied my shoes of water, dried my trousers with my hanky, then sat in the van and calmed myself. Ted Faulter would have to wait; right now I had to *sell* something! Okay – the first lead was blown, but there were still two more to go and these *had* to succeed.

Firstly, though, a little preparation was called for.

I started the van, drove back along the Fulham Road, and stopped at an electrical shop. There I bought four 13-amp plugs and a screw-driver, then spent a few minutes putting plugs on the two food-mixers and the two vacuum cleaners, and at the same time checked all the appliances to make sure all their bits and pieces were there.

Right, now I'm ready for you, Mrs Barry of Bermondsey. I am going to flog you a Zip Food Mixer if it's the last thing I do!

By God, it nearly was.

Paradise Road, I discovered, lay as close to the River Thames as you could get without falling in it – and there may well be those who hold the opinion that it's a great pity it didn't lie just that little bit closer.

Situated across-river from Wapping Docks it is not, to say the least, one of East London's most salubrious thoroughfares; to say the most, it's a flaming slum.

Oh, I thought, as I turned into it. Whoever christened it Paradise Road must either have had a brutal sense of humour or lost his marbles.

I drove slowly down it, scanning the festering terraced houses for number 226, the prospect of entering any one of them was enough to turn the stomach.

The cobbled street was full of kids, millions of 'em, swinging on lamp posts, throwing stones, chalking on the pavements, beating each other up, and as I drove up they stopped what they were doing and stared at me with a malevolent interest that sent shivers of presentiment up my spine.

By gum, this lot would need watching.

I found 226 and drew to the curb, and even before I'd cut the engine they were surrounding me six deep, as threatening as triffids. Right, I thought, it's time for a bit of child psychology. I'd run into a similar situation in Liverpool's infamous Scotland Road while working for Ritebuy and knew exactly how to handle it. You get the leader of the pack on your side through blatant bribery and *he* controls the mob while you're in the house. Simple.

With a confident, friendly smile, I opened the door and climbed out, right into the thick of it.

'Hi, fellas . . . who's the leader around here?'

Eighty-four voices yelled, 'ME!'

Oh, blimey . . .

'What do you want in our street, mister?' demanded an acrimonious voice.

'Let's get 'im!'

'Rip 'is wing mirrors orf!'

'Get the windscreen wipers!'

'Now, lads . . . LADS! STOP! Hey, leave that mirror alone, you little . . .'

'Fuckin' make me!'

'Now, listen . . . LISTEN!' I pulled a pound note out of my pocket and waved it aloft. 'LOOK! LISTEN!' The sight of folding money did the trick; the noise abated. 'Okay, now listen to me . . . you all know Mrs Barry, don't you?'

There was a muttered chorus of agreement.

'Well, I've come to deliver something for Mrs Barry – and I'm sure she wouldn't be very pleased if you damaged my van while I was in her house, now would she?'

I got silence which was better than I expected.

'Of course she wouldn't. All right, tell me, does Mrs Barry have any children?'

'Yeh, ten,' sniffed a kid with a patch on his left eye.

I gaped at him, 'Ten?'

'Yeh – he's one of 'em.' He pointed to a scowling red-haired kid in a blue football jersey.

'Oh, really? Come here, son . . . what's your name?'

'Mickey,' he scowled, his beady eyes on the pound note.

'All right, Mickey, now listen, your mother has asked me to bring something for her . . .'

'Warrisit?'

'It's a food mixer . . . for making cakes and things. I'm going to show her how it works, so I'll be in the house for quite a while, and I want you fellas to look after my van while I'm inside, what d'you say?'

'What's that for?' he asked, meaning the pound note.

'This . . . is for you lads . . .'

A cheer went up.

'. . . *IF* the van isn't harmed while I'm in the house! Understand?'

'Can we have it now?'

'No – when I come out.'

'You won't give it to us.'

'All right, tell you what I'll do . . .' I tore the pound note in two, drawing an appalled gasp from the assembly. 'Here you are, you keep one half, I'll keep the other. If the van's unharmed when I come out, I'll give you this other half – okay?'

'Okay,' he muttered grudgingly.

'Good – now you're in charge. But this money is for sweets for *all* of you, so you've all got to look after the van.'

'You wannit washed, mister?' asked Eye Patch. 'I'll do it for a quid.'

'No, thanks.'

'Fifty pence, then?'

'No thanks . . .'

Now came a deluge of offers. 'Forty pence . . . thirty . . . twenty . . . ten!'

'NO, THANK YOU! All right, now clear off, you guys . . .'

I pushed through them to the back of the van and got out the Mark One mixer, then, securely locking up, headed for the front door and gave the knocker a good one.

Several moments passed, then the door opened. She was beautiful – fourteen stone of emancipated glamour in hair curlers and a filthy pinny, a baby on her hip and a fag in her mouth, one eye closed against the smoke. 'Yers?'

'Mrs Barry?'

'Yers?'

'My name is Tobin, I'm from Zip Electrics. You sent in a coupon for a food mixer . . .'

'Oh, blimey, yers! I'd forgot all abart it. Come on in, you've come just at the right time, I was goin' to do some bakin'. 'Ere, you kids, you leave that bleedin' van alone! Mickey, you touch that van an' I'll batter the daylights outta yer!'

Now, that's what I called child psychology!

She about-turned and went down the hall, and, drawing a last lungful of fresh air, I followed.

To get to the kitchen I had to pass through the rear living-room and I'd have given anything not to. It was unbelievable. Picking my way between a jam butty and a baby's potty, I stepped over a three-year-old boy who was whittling away at the table leg with a bread knife, circumnavigated a pup who was eating a sausage roll, and entered the kitchen.

My stomach lurched.

'Sorry about the mess,' she sniffed, dropping an inch of ash on the baby's foot. 'One of the youngsters is in bed sick, so I'm a bit be'ind today. Where d'you want to put it?'

Back in the van right now, I thought, wondering how long I could keep holding my breath.

There was a table against the wall with a wall-socket above it. 'That'll be fine, if we could sort of... clear it a bit.'

'I'll get the kids to do it. Leslie – go an' get Anne, Mary and Freddy out of the street – go on!'

I put the carton on the table and began unpacking the mixer, and was just finishing when the place exploded with kids. Christ, there were dozens of them.

' 'Ere, you lot, clear this table for the gentleman . . . stick those dishes in the sink. Freddy, *don't* touch that bread with yer filthy 'ands . . .'

It was bedlam; noise pulverized the ears.

'I wus just going to make a coupla cakes!' shouted Mrs B. 'Does it do cakes?'

'It does everything! It's got a three-speed motor.'

'Fancy!'

'And a unique double-beater action.'

'Coo!'

'Plus an egg whisk and a dough hook.'

'A what?'

'A dough hook!'

'Thought you said door hook,' she laughed. 'Good, certainly looks a nice machine. Well, we may as well try it out right now, hey?'

My jaw dropped. 'You mean . . . with real food?'

'Certainly. That's what it's for, isn't it?'

'Well, yes, but . . .'

Oh, rotten hell . . . how is it these situations never come up in training sessions? The customer isn't *supposed* to want to use it right away!

'Right . . .' she said determindedly. 'Here, Anne – take the baby! Freddy – get the flour out of that cupboard! And some eggs and castor sugar and a packet of currants! Mary – get two packets of butter out of the fridge . . . now, where did I put those scales . . . ?'

I watched, numbed, as the ingredients were weighed and assembled. It was no longer my mixer – the hordes had taken over. Self-raising flour flew all over the place as Mrs B. weighed out twenty ounces of it and chucked it into the mixer bowl, following it with a small mountain of rock-hard butter and castor sugar, enough, it seemed to me, for a dozen cakes.

'Right!' she announced. 'Ready for creaming!'

'Oh . . .'

'What do I do – just turn this knob?'

'Er, yes . . . turn it to number one.'

She switched it on. A cheer went up. It actually worked!

Mrs B. turned to me with a grin. 'Ooh, this is better, it takes me hours to do this by hand. Oh, I've got to have this little beauty.'

My God, I was actually going to make a sale!

For several minutes the mixer ground away, the motor whirring and surging as though in great pain as it laboriously churned the great bowlful of ingredients into a crumbly mess. Knowing nothing at all about mixers I couldn't tell whether the noise was normal, but I had a prickle of premonition it was being asked to do too much. The Super De Luxe model – okay, that looked as though it could cope with this amount of stuff, but the puny Mark One . . .

'Mary – pass me those eggs!' demanded the jubilant Mrs Barry.

One by one she cracked the eggs and dropped them into the bowl, a disturbing change of motor-pitch accompanying each additional strain on the beaters.

'Freddy . . . stop stickin' your filthy fingers in that sugar! Mary, leave those bleedin' currants alone! Anne . . . the baby's got an egg!' She peered into the bowl. 'Right, that lot's about done, now for the fruit!'

In went eight tons of currants.

The motor gave a shocked cough, the beaters faltered. I broke out in a cold sweat.

'Er . . . Mrs Barry . . .' I started to say.

'We need more power!' she declared, and turned the switch to top speed.

What happened next was pure Laurel and Hardy. The motor gave a shriek like it had been goosed and the beaters went berserk, took off at incredible speed, began chucking out great handfuls of cake-mix all over the kitchen, while at the same time the mixer broke into a kangaroo dance and leapt across the table . . . a-dump-dee-dump-dee dump . . . heading inexorably for the edge.

Splot! Freddy copped a faceful of cake-mix and started to yell.

Splat! Anne got a dollop in the eye.

Splut! I collected a blob in the flies.

Pandemonium erupted – the motor screaming, kids screaming, me yelling at Mrs Barry to switch the thing off,

Mrs Barry yelling at me to switch it off . . . and a blizzard of cake-mix flying everywhere.

I made a lunge for the machine but too late . . . a-dump-dee-dump-dee . . . CRASH!

It hit the floor and shattered into eighty-four pieces.

'OhhhhhHHHHHHHHHH!' roared Mrs Barry, scraping up a handful of mix and slinging it at me. 'NOW look what you've done! Look at all the food you've wasted . . . ! You'll have to pay for this!'

'Yes . . . yes, I will,' I stammered, down on the floor, shovelling bits of mixer into the box. 'You overloaded it, you know . . . you put too much in the bowl, Mrs Barry!'

'And 'ow the 'ell was *I* to know it wouldn't take it! *You're* supposed to be the bloody expert! You owe me a quid for all this! And who's goin' to clean up all this mess?'

I scrambled to my feet, stuck a pound note in her hand and got out fast, seen off with a hail of abuse from the kitchen.

''Ow about the other 'alf of that nicker, mister?' demanded Mickey, out on the pavement.

Cursing, I handed it over and the gang dispersed with a whoop.

I flung the remains of the mixer into the back of the van and threw myself into the driver's seat, hitting sixty before I'd reached the end of the street.

Mad . . . MAD! It couldn't have happened! Nobody could be cursed with this sort of luck. Then suspicion began to dawn. Had I been given a faulty machine? Had Ted Faulter struck again with a bum mixer?

Well, there'd be no way of proving it now.

I drove down to the Embankment and parked for a while, cleaned the cake mix off my suit and got myself together for the next – and last – call of the day. Marvellous . . . Russell Tobin, the hot-shot salesman, two disasters out of two.

Well, by God, there wasn't going to be a third.

Mrs Diamond of Wimbledon was *going* to buy a Super De Luxe vacuum cleaner.

Even if I had to pay for the bloody thing myself!

CHAPER SIX

Grim with determination, I raced up Putney Hill and entered the quiet suburban splendour of Wimbledon Park Side, a welcome oasis of order and grandeur after the grot and turmoil of Paradise Road. Its solid respectability a balm to my nerves, its monetary promise a bolster to my flagging hopes, I was a new man even before I turned into the gates of Clifton House – and a damn-sight newer afterwards.

It was magnificent; a hundred thousand quidsworth of yellow-brick Georgian bezaz, fronted by half an acre of perfect emerald lawns and Percy Thrower rose-beds.

The only thing I didn't like about it were the half dozen cars parked in the driveway. She had company – and to a salesman that spelled trouble. I'd come at the wrong time.

Well, I thought, as I parked the van, no doubt she'd let me know if it wasn't convenient. Ladies who live in this kind of house are never backward at speaking their minds.

I got the Mark One cleaner out of the van and crunched up the driveway to the front door, wondering, as I rang the door-chimes, why a woman such as this would be interested in a cheap vacuum cleaner.

Then again, who could fathom the thinking of the rich? Being careful with their lolly was probably how they got rich in the first place.

Footsteps approached the door, and a woman's voice called out in bantering tone, as though she were completing a conversation, '. . . so don't ask him, see if I care! I'll ask Hymie myself. No, I won't – I'll *tell* him, already!'

Laughing, she opened the door, the smile draining from her face as she took in the vacuum cleaner carton and the Zip van parked behind me.

She was a small, good-looking woman in her thirties, dark-haired, vivacious, and beautifully dressed in a long brown velvet skirt and cream silk blouse, with an Arab's ransom of gold and diamonds on her wrists, fingers, neck, ears and breasts. She looked a tough little bird – Jewish and formidable, and in the next breath proved it.

Realizing who I was, she rolled her eyes despairingly and sighed, 'Oh, Christ, what a time to come, You should've called! I'm in the middle of a hen-party.'

'I'm s . . . sorry, Mrs Diamond, I didn't realize. I'll come back later, then . . .'

I started to move away but a thought suddenly struck her. 'No! No, it's all right . . . come on in.' She gave me a twisted smile. 'You can entertain the girls with a demonstration.'

My heart sank.

'Come in,' she commanded, 'and take your shoes off, this carpet cost a fortune. You should have used the tradesmen's entrance round the back.'

'I'm sorry, I . . .'

'And for Godsake stop apologizing, you give a bad impression. Come on, this way.'

Well, I was a bundle of nerves before I started! The situation couldn't have been worse – a roomful of women *and* her to contend with. I mean, the odds against 'switching' a bird like Diamond were so long they were out of sight!

Dolefully I followed her along the hall, pending doom a foregone conclusion. She led me into a huge, lavishly furnished drawing-room of sumptuous settees and sparkling chandeliers, gilded mirrors and priceless antiques, occupied by a dozen women all nattering away eighteen to the dozen and sounding just like a gaggle of hens in a farmyard.

'Girls, girls!' announced Mrs Diamond, clapping her hands for silence, 'I've got a lovely surprise for you . . . this is Mr . . .' she turned to me.

'T . . . Tobin,' I stammered, hating myself for doing it but I felt such a berk standing there in my stockinged feet.

'Mr Turpin from Zip Electrics who's come to give us a demonstration of a vacuum cleaner.'

There was a twitter of approval and a general surge to get closer for a better look.

'Who the heck's Zip Electrics, Rose?' asked another tough-looking bird in a red silk trouser suit, an ivory cigarette-holder clamped between her teeth.

Rose Diamond shrugged eloquently. 'Who knows? I saw their ad. in the paper for a cheap cleaner and thought it'd do fine for the games room. I don't need anything heavy in there.'

Oh, brother . . . this really was my day. There went *all* hope of doing a switch.

Rose Diamond turned to me. 'So go ahead – give us a dem.'

'In here?' I asked, surprised, because I didn't think she'd let me anywhere near this magnificent, long-piled white carpet that must have cost eight trillion pounds a square foot.

'Sure in here. Come on, get it unpacked.'

I knelt down and got the thing out of its carton. A buzz of comment, mostly critical, greeted its appearance.

'Looks a bit tinny, Rose.'

'So – what d'you expect for thirteen pounds – an industrial cleaner? It's only for fluff in the games room.'

'You'll be lucky if it lasts three weeks. Take my advice, never buy anything cheap, it's never worth it.'

'Er . . .' I said, wishing the carpet-pile would swallow me, wishing I'd never come, wishing I'd never heard of bloody Zip Electrics. 'Is there a wall-socket handy, Mrs. Diamond?'

'Behind that settee.'

I pulled the flex out of the machine to its fullest extent and made a move for the wall.

'Hey!' she exclaimed. 'Mind the vase on that side-table, it's very valuable!'

'Yes, Mrs Diamond.'

Carefully I trailed the wire around the small table, which was standing at the side of the settee, and dropped down behind the settee to put in the plug. And here, fresh horror awaited me.

The plug I'd put on the cleaner was a modern 13-amp flat-pin, but the socket in the wall was an old 15-amp round-pin!

'Godallbloodymighty . . .' I cursed to myself. Would *nothing* go right this day.

I stood up. 'I'll have to go out to the van, Mrs Diamond, I need a screw driver.'

She shrugged. 'So – go.'

I went . . . and came back, dreading the thought of entering that room again.

'Are you going to be long?' she asked me irritably. 'We can't wait all day.'

'No, just a couple of seconds, Mrs Diamond . . .'

I got down behind the settee again, took the plug off the flex, and shoved the bare wires into the wall socket.

'Ready, now,' I announced.

The babble subsided.

I cleared my throat. 'Well . . . here we have the Zip Electrics Vacuum Cleaner Mark One . . .'

'Is there a Mark Two?' asked the trouble-maker in the red cat-suit.

'Er, no, not precisely . . .'

'So why d'you call this the Mark One?'

They all laughed at her – and at my dilemma. Good game, this, it was called Rip The Salesman To Shreds, and they all joined in with gusto.

'Makes it sound more important, doesn't it, sugar?' snided a huge woman in a silver lamé blouse. 'Well, it certainly looks as though it needs all the help it can get!'

'Go on, switch it on, Mr Turpin,' teased another. 'Cover your ears, girls, the power will be deafening!'

'Yes, well . . .' I said, forcing myself to go through the spiel, '. . . as you can see, it has a light-weight ultra-flex hose for easy manoeuvrability . . .'

'They're no good,' opined Cat Suit. 'They split too easily. Take a tip from me, Rose, don't ever buy an ultra-flex hose.'

'Then . . . there are these two extension tubes,' I staggered on, my guts in knots, marvelling that I was standing there talking all this rubbish, '. . . very useful for reaching high curtains and pelmets . . . this carpet attachment with a brush and alternative easy-glide action . . . this upholstery nozzle . . . and this crevice nozzle . . .'

Mrs Diamond tutted impatiently. 'Yes, yes, well just get on with it. Switch it on and let's see how it sucks.'

'Y . . . yes, certainly . . .'

I prodded the start button with my toe.

Nothing happened.

Awful, ear-tearing silence filled the room.

'Hey . . . ter*rific*!' exclaimed Silver Lamé Blouse. 'Now, that's what I *call* a quiet cleaner!'

A gale of laughter and a barrage of cracks ensued.

'Fan*tastic* little machine! You know, you'd hardly know it was running.'

'Dangerous, though, you'd never know whether it was on or off. You might get home and find it had swallowed all your carpets!'

'What's the matter with it?' demanded Mrs Diamond.

'I . . . I think the wires might have come out of the wall.'

'Well, go look!'

I did. I crouched down and gave the wires a wiggle . . . and immediately the room erupted with noise. My God, what a racket. It sounded like the Concorde starting up in a tin shed.

A scoffing cheer went up from the women and they backed away from it in mock terror, as though it was a time bomb about to explode.

'Oh, my *God* . . . !' exclaimed Rose Diamond, clamping her hands over her ears.

I leapt from behind the settee intending to shut the thing off, but Cat Suit yelled. 'Okay – so it's deafening, but does it suck?'

'Of course it . . .' I stuck my hand over the end of the nozzle, expecting my skin to fly up the spout, '. . . sucks.'

Oh, Jesus . . . nothing was happening. I mean, there wasn't enough power there to suck up a feather.

Cat Suit shrieked with laughter.

What could have happened? Had the impeller fallen off

the motor? Maybe that's why it was making such a racket!

'Here . . .' goaded Cat Suit, ripping a Kleenex tissue into shreds and dropping them on the carpet. 'Pick those up!'

Sick with despair I lowered the nozzle to the ground and ran it up to the first piece of tissue. It was still lying there a minute later.

The girls were in pleats, falling about, tears streaming down their faces.

'Shut it off . . . shut it off!' bellowed Mrs Diamond, helpless with laughter, her mascara running down her cheeks.

I gave the machine a kick in the head, ceasing its terrible roar.

'Oh . . . oh, my God,' gasped Mrs Diamond, clutching her ribs. 'Oh, that was wonderful, Mr Turpin, thank you so much, I'll take two . . .'

She collapsed with laughter again and fell against Silver Blouse who was doubled up, clutching her stomach. They were *all* doubled up and helpless, as only a gang of girls can be when they really get the giggles.

Gradually they subsided, wiped their eyes, blew their noses, broke out in a fresh paroxysm, then finally came to rest.

Mrs Diamond looked at me and shrugged. 'What can I say except . . . it's rubbish, get it out of my house!'

They all laughed.

'Mrs Diamond, to be honest . . . I think we've got a bad cleaner here.'

Fresh gales of laughter.

'No . . . no, I mean, there's something wrong with it. It shouldn't make that noise. I think the impeller might have fallen off . . . or something. That's why it's not sucking.'

'Well, whatever it is . . . goodbye, Mr Turpin.'

'Mrs Diamond . . . look, I've got another cleaner in the van, a much better one, It's the Super De Luxe model. Would you let me show it to you?'

Her eyes narrowed. 'How much?'

'Well . . . a bit more expensive, but it really is a wonderful cleaner.'

Cat Suit leapt in. 'Oh, go on, Rosie, let him bring it in. I haven't had such a good laugh since Hymie fell in the pond at George's barmitzvah.'

With a smile, bowing to popular demand, Mrs Diamond gave me the nod. 'All right, go get it.'

I was off like a shot. All was not yet lost. A good dem. on the Super and I might just pull it off. In fact, if I was able to impress all those women it might be difficult for Rose Diamond to say no!

I got the Super out of the van and hurried back before they all went off the boil. Hope soared as I removed the cleaner from its box and heard the approving comments.

'Better,' stated Cat Suit authoritatively, expert on everything, this one, except minding her own business.

'How much?' demanded Rose.

'Well, it's . . .' I dived behind the settee and began taking off the plug, '. . . naturally you'd expect to pay a *bit* more for this because it's the Super De Luxe model, Mrs Diamond . . .'

'You wouldn't be Jewish by any chance, would you?' she asked, making them laugh again. '*How* much more, Mr Turpin?'

I rammed the wires in the holes and stood up. 'Now, just listen to *this* motor, ladies . . .'

I kicked the switch.

By heaven, it sounded terrific, immensely powerful but properly subdued, that sweet, true sound of a motor in tip-top form.

'There . . .' I beamed. '*Now* we'll dispose of that Kleenex.'

I lowered the nozzle to the floor.

Swup! . . . Swup! . . . Swup! . . . up the pipe it flew.

'How about that!' I grinned, happy as hell that at last something was going right. 'And just look at the way it's attacking this long-piled carpet. Did you ever see a more powerful cleaner than this? The suction is fan*tas*tic!'

In fact, it was so bloody fantastic I could hardly push the nozzle through the pile. I pulled . . . pushed . . . but the damn thing was stuck. The pile was jammed solid up the pipe!

'Here, let me,' insisted Cat Suit, snatching the hose out of my hand. 'This needs a woman's touch. We do this every day of our lives. You need a bit of . . . *beef* behind it! AaauuuuuUUUUUHHHHHH!'

She gave it a shove and nearly ruptured herself. 'My God, it's stuck!'

Rose Diamond's jaw dropped. 'My carpet! Marion don't . . .'

But Marion already was. Unable to push it forward, her automatic reaction was to try to pull it backwards, and, like a fisherman landing a four-ton shark, she gave one almighty heave with the intention of dragging the nozzle away from the pile.

But at the very moment of the heave, Rose Diamond let out a bellow of protest and kicked the switch to 'off', instantly killing the suction.

Up came the nozzle in a scything arc, straight at my nuts. With the superhuman speed a man can engender only when he's about to get it in the balls, I spun away and got it in the arse, a full-blooded blow that shot me forward into the arms of Silver Blouse, who stepped back on the foot of a tiny creature in a pink frock, who lashed out and hit a big momma in a blue frock in the tits, who let go a horrified yell and promptly sat down on the priceless vase sitting on the fragile little antique side-table and shattered the whole fucking kit and caboodle into a billion trillion pieces.

Rose Diamond's demented wail spiralled like the baying of a love-lorn wolf, then exploded in a great tearing bellow of white-hot rage . . . and then the upholstery nozzle smacked into the back of my head with the velocity of a twelve-inch shell.

'GET OUT OF MY HOUSE, YOU . . . GET OUT! . . . GET OUT!'

'Mrs Diamond, please, I . . .'

Whop! I got the crevice nozzle in the guts.

'OUT! . . . OUT! . . . OUT! . . . AND TAKE THIS *GARBAGE* WITH YOU!'

I snatched up the two cleaners, and in a tangle of pipes and hose and flex and attachments fled for the front door.

Bang! It closed behind me, then quickly opened again and my shoes came hurtling out.

'I'll sue you!' she screamed, shaking her fist at me. 'I'll ruin you!'

THUD! The door slammed shut with awful finality.

I hobbled to the van and slung the festering cleaners into the back.

Ruin me? You're one day too late, love, I thought.

I've already done it myself!

CHAPTER SEVEN

I didn't go home immediately, I couldn't face Dennis, so I just drove aimlessly. Three failures out of three! It was calamitous. I'd have to resign, of course. The shattered Mark One food mixer would cost me all the commission I was likely to earn in three months at the rate I was selling, so I saw no point in going back to Zip. I'd return the van first thing in the morning and keep on walking.

'And do what?' I asked myself.

'Chuck yourself in the Thames' seemed nicely appropriate right then. One thing is certain, Tobin, you can forget this selling lark, you've lost the touch, son. Christ, you didn't even sell the *Mark One* of anything – even though they sent the coupon in for a dem!

Try as I might to console myself that it was the fault of bum appliances and lack of preparation, that this could never happen again because in future I'd thoroughly check the appliances before I left Zip, it didn't work; and so it was in a mood of black despondency that I found myself walking into the *Red Dog* pub just off Wimbledon Common without realizing I'd even stopped the van.

'Evening,' nodded the barman.

I frowned at him 'It is?' I looked at my watch. Good God, it was nearly seven o'clock. I must have been driving round in circles for an hour.

He looked at me closely. 'You all right, sir?'

'Hm? Yes, fine.'

'What'll it be, sir?'

I put my hand in my pocket and drew out my last pound note. 'A large vodka and tonic, please.'

I got the drink and fifty pence change – enough for another and then that was it, I'd have to go home.

I turned away from the bar and looked for a vacant table. The pub was pretty full on this warm summer evening, but there was a space on a banquette seat against the wall.

As I walked over I subconsciously registered the woman I was going to sit next to, but that was all. I was in no mood for the hunt. She was good-looking in an unstartling way, good cheekbones, nice grey-green eyes and well-formed mouth, but all a bit colourless without make-up. In a single sweep I got the impression of slimness – even thinness – beneath a red and blue floral dress, blondish hair tied back in a pony tail, and good legs, though when they're crossed you can never be sure.

As I approached, she glanced up and caught my eyes, held them for a brief moment with the interest any woman would give any man who was about to sit beside her, then, as I sat down, she looked away and terminated the relationship.

I got out my cigarettes and lit one, drank some vodka and was soon lost in thought about the future.

It was some minutes later that I became aware that she was fruitlessly flicking a flintless lighter in an attempt to light her cigarette. I picked mine up and offered her a flame which she accepted, her eyes coming up from it to thank me.

'Thank you,' she said softly, a nice, gentle voice.

'They tend to work better with a flint.' I said.

She smiled and turned away, reaching for her drink. Dubonnet, I think. I watched her raise it to her mouth, now realizing she had a beautiful profile, nice straight nose, sculptured mouth, and small firm chin. With make-up she'd look a knockout.

Casually I looked her over. She was about thirty, I reckoned . . . secretary type. Not too flush – the dress and shoes were good but not expensive and she wore very little jewellery. She'd probably popped in for a quick drink on her way back from work, she had that dishevelled commuter look about her.

Vaguely I wondered if she was waiting for someone, though it was the type of pub – almost rural, so close to the common – that women did frequent solo on the way back from work. I didn't give it much thought.

Moments passed. Suddenly she bent down for her handbag that was tucked under the seat and got to her feet, probably heading for the loo, and as she squeezed past me and between the two small tables I caught the drift of her perfume.

Beautiful . . . delicate and sexy.

I watched her move across the room, her figure as good as it had promised to be, marvellous legs and a lovely bum, perhaps a little thin on top but it didn't matter.

I drank some more vodka and studied the inmates, a cheerful lot enjoying a beautiful evening and a well-earned drink after a day's toil in the city. I was glad I'd chosen this pub; I was beginning to feel better.

When she reappeared I almost didn't recognize her. She'd released her hair from its pony-tail and put on a bit of make-up, accentuating her oval eyes and the perfect curve of her mouth which now lifted in a little smile as she squeezed between the tables and sat down.

'Thank you,' she said again, as though I'd done something for her.

Wooomff! I got a clout of her perfume again in a delayed wake and went funny in the head. If ever there was a sucker for scent it's Russell Tobin.

'Wow . . .' I growled, giving a delicate sniff, and she turned and grinned. 'Mind if I ask what it's called?'

She thought about it for a second, then said, 'Moment Supreme.'

'That's no lie. I may never be the same again.'

Her lips curved in a beautiful smile. 'That's the general idea.'

I shook my head. 'It's not fair, you know, we fellas have got no defence against that sort of thing. You can bring us down at forty paces, no effort at all. It's a bit like trying to fight a boxer with a ten foot reach.'

She arched a provocative brow. 'Then perhaps you shouldn't try to fight it.'

Aye aye . . .

The old ticker gave a jump and the pulse-rate moved up a touch. Was there a game afoot?

But in the same brief instant desolation washed over me. I was stony-broke! How could I join the game with only fifty lousy pence in my pocket? Oh, curses . . .

Astutely she picked up my hesitation and her brow clouded in a frown. 'Sorry, did I say something . . .'

'Oh, no . . . no, it's . . .'

'You have the same worried look you had when you came in. Are you in trouble?'

I smiled. 'No, not trouble trouble . . . not the police or anything like that. I've just had a lousy day, that's all.'

She gave a wry laugh. 'Welcome to the club.'

'Oh, you, too?'

'Hm hm.' She picked up her drink and swallowed some.

'Would you like a cigarette?'

She took one, put it between her beautiful lips and accepted my light. 'Thank you.'

'My name's Tobin . . . Russ Tobin.'

'Mine's Kate Reinhardt.'

'I'm very pleased to meet you.'

She smiled. 'You may not be, I'm not very good company tonight.'

'You've really got troubles, hm?'

'Oh . . .' she gave a shrug. 'Man trouble. It's not the end of the world, I suppose, but . . .'

'You'll need a few days to get over it.'

'Something like that. What's your trouble?'

'Mine? I'm broke.'

'Oh. Well at least that's not terminal.'

'No, just damned uncomfortable. I'm not used to it and I don't quite know how to cope.'

'How about working your way out of it?'

'I tried that today. It was a terrible disaster.'

She gave me a critical eye. 'Try it again tomorrow. It does take time to pick up the habit, you know.'

‘Ooh,wait on, don’t get the wrong idea. I’m no rich lay-about who’s just blown his trust fund. I’ve been hard at it since I was sixteen. No, what I meant was . . .’

Well, I told her about it – about arriving from Dublin and finding the cupboard bare . . . and about how I’d earned the money in the first place . . . which took us on to Majorca, then Africa . . . and so on and so on and suddenly it was time for another drink and the depression swamped me again.

‘Kate,’ I sighed, ‘there is nothing I would like better right now than to buy you a drink, but . . .’ I slapped the fifty pence down on the table, ‘. . . *that* is the sum total of my worldly wealth, so help me.’

She giggled. ‘I think it’s funny.’

‘Thank you, I can use the sympathy.’

She reached down for her handbag and took out a wallet . . . an extremely fat wallet. From a thick wad of notes she peeled a fiver and tossed it on to the table. ‘Here – go get some drinks.’

‘No. At least, I will, but I’ll pay for mine.’

She rolled her eyes exasperatedly. ‘Oh, for heaven’s sake . . . this is 1977 not 1877.’

‘Don’t care.’

She sighed dramatically. ‘All right, but go, I’m dying of thirst.’

When I got back with the drinks she raised her glass and looked at me over the rim. ‘We’ll win, you know, we Women’s Libbers.’

‘So will we Men’s Libbers, so in fact nothing will change.’

‘I’ll drink to that.’ She did so and put down her glass. Then she took out the wallet, showed it to me. ‘Severance pay. I got fired today.’

‘Oh, dear. That in *addition* to man troubles?’

‘The first was the result of the second.’

‘Oh. He was your boss?’

‘You’re very astute. Yes, the bastard.’

‘So what happened?’

‘Things got messy. His wife called in at the office and

decided I represented too much temptation for him and too much competition for her.'

I grinned. 'And did you?'

'Guilty on both counts,' she laughed. 'Mind you, nothing had actually *happened* between us.'

'Of course not. What a preposterous suggestion.'

'You don't believe me!'

'Well I was picturing myself in his place and . . .'

'And?'

'Well, either he was a man of steel or off his chump . . .'

She threw back her head and laughed. 'We'll say no more.'

'What sort of a job was it, Kate?'

'Photographer's assistant. He has a studio in Chelsea.'

'Ah ha . . .'

'And what does that mean?'

'Nothing,' I grinned. 'Except the wife's attitude is just that leetle bit easier to understand, what with . . . you know, *darkrooms* lying around all nice and handy . . .'

'What a disgusting suggestion.'

'. . . and maybe the odd bit of *modelling* that needed to be done . . .'

'I don't think I like you, Russ Tobin.'

'Oh, Kate, these aren't my thoughts, they're *hers*! Heaven forbid anything so . . . so unprincipled should freely enter my mind.'

She was giving me a very old-fashioned look which suddenly blossomed into a capitulative grin. 'As a matter of fact they were her very suspicions.'

'Shame, you obviously enjoyed it . . . the photographic business, I mean. So – what are you going to do now?'

She sighed. 'Probably shoot myself.'

'I was thinking of the Thames. Would you care to join me?'

She made a face. 'We hardly know each other! I couldn't do it with a complete stranger. Besides, I swim like a fish.'

'Oh well, leave it for the time being, maybe something'll come to us. Have a cigarette, it'll help us think.'

As she blew out pretty smoke, I asked her, 'Where do

you live?'

She pointed over her shoulder. 'Just off Putney Hill. It's tiny but all mine.'

'A flat?'

'Yes . . . about the size of a tea caddy – bedroom, lounge-cum-kitchen, bathroom.'

'You live alone? . . . and please don't misinterpret the question, I'm not fishing.'

She smiled. 'I don't mind, I'm a big girl now, I can handle it. Yes, I live alone. Time was when I didn't, but . . .' she gave a shrug. 'C'est la vie.'

'You were married?'

'Hm mm,' she nodded. 'About eight thousand years ago. How about you?'

'No.'

'Girl friend?'

'No.'

She frowned at me.

'Like I said, I've been away for two years.'

'Ah.'

And that was that out of the way.

'Tell me about your boarding house,' she said, taking a drink. 'Is it comfortable?'

'Homely and wholesome. It's run by an Italian family named Carlotti who have four kids . . . Dotty, Spotty, Grotty and Potty.'

She shrieked with laughter, quickly clamping a hand over her mouth. 'I'm sorry, but that's ridiculous.'

'Yes, isn't it. There are some other odd-ball guests in the house besides me . . . a weirdo actor, a travelling salesman, a waiter, a taxi driver . . .'

'Sounds like fun. What's the food like?'

I shrugged. 'Don't know, I've never eaten there. I only moved in last night.'

'What do you like to eat?'

'Me? Anything . . . almost everything.'

'Do you like steak?'

'Love it.'

She paused as though hesitating, then said quietly, 'I've got two porterhouse at home . . . would you?'

I smiled at her. 'Kate, that's the nicest thing I've heard all day.'

'Come on,' she said, quickly gathering up her handbag. 'I've been dying to practise on someone for months.'

CHAPTER EIGHT

She drove a little red Morris 1100; I followed in the van, but had barely got going when we arrived.

'Jurst a*dore* your automobile,' she cracked in American accent, locking her car. 'My, I'll bet you *really* pull the girls with that, honey.'

'Very funny. Don't you know it's cruel to mock the afflicted?'

We climbed to the third floor in a mini-elevator, our sudden awareness of being alone in a very confined space resulting in an awkward silence which she finally broke with a laugh.

'I wonder why it is that people stop talking when they get into a lift?'

'The shrinks would probably say . . . oh.'

The lift stopped and the doors opened.

'It's to the left,' she said. '343. What would the psychiatrists say?'

'Oh . . . something about the confinement of space causing a heightened awareness of intimate juxtaposition between the sexes.'

'Would they really?' she grinned. 'Is that what happened between us?'

'Wouldn't be at all surprised.'

She opened the door with a key and went in, putting on lights as she made her way down a narrow hall, to the living room, passing two closed doors on the left.

'Bathroom,' she informed me, tapping the second of the doors.

'Ta.'

The living room was not large but it was very nicely

decorated in browns and yellows and oranges. Two large windows overlooked the street, or more correctly overlooked the foliage of tall silver birch trees growing in the pavement fifty feet from the building, resulting in the impression that the flat aspired to a sylvan rather than concrete setting.

'Very nice,' I remarked.

'Thank you,' she said, cutting left to a tiny kitchen psychologically separated from the living room in a recessed alcove. 'What were you drinking?'

'Vodka tonic . . . but don't worry if you haven't got it.'

'I've got it. Put on some music.'

I crossed to a stereo unit built into a shelf system and ran an eye over her collection of cassettes. There was a bit of everything from Wagner to Wings – but the majority was as I'd expected – Jack Jones, Vic Damone, Sinatra, Streisand, Andy Williams.

The lady was a romantic.

With a smile to myself, I picked out a Jack Jones with a big band backing, romantic yet sufficiently swingy for the time of the evening, something to get the fingers snapping rather than the bed-springs twanging.

As the opening bars of 'Without Her' began filling the room, she popped her head out of the alcove and gave me a pleased grin. 'Oh, very clever. How did you know it was my favourite?'

'It sounded like you.'

'*Adore* that man.'

She came out with the drinks, put them on a low glass table in front of a floral settee, and sat down, curling her legs under her. I sat at the opposite end and got my cigarettes out.

'No,' she commanded, pointing to an onyx box on the table. 'Smoke those.'

We got a couple going, drank our drinks, commented on the music, the singer, the next singer, had another drink, put on Sinatra, talked about him, had another drink, and time sped.

Suddenly she glanced at her watch and did a double-take. 'I don't believe it . . . it's ten o'clock! You must be starved! I'd better do the steaks.'

'Can I help?'

'Yes, put on another tape and come and talk to me.'

With Andy Williams under way, I went into the kitchen, straddled a stool at a bar counter and watched her prepare the meal. As I may have said before, there are few things more pleasurable than to watch an attractive, graceful, deft, feminine female flit about a kitchen in her little pinny getting a meal together. This is her domain and she is queen. Trouble is, they get to look so damn sexy, the last thing you want them to do is get a meal together.

'How's your drink?' she asked, suddenly turning from the cooker and catching me at it. 'Hey . . . what was going through your mind?'

I grinned. 'Oh . . . I was just sitting here thinking how good you look in your cute little pinny.'

A smile tugged at the corner of her mouth. 'Anything else – or just the pinny?'

'Now, would I entertain thoughts like that?'

'You're damn right. You're a fella, aren't you?'

I held up two fingers, Scout-wise. 'I cannot tell a lie – yes, I am a fella.'

She picked up my glass and took it to the fridge for a refill. 'I thought as much. The moment I saw you walk into the pub, I though to myself *that* is a fella. You can't always be sure, you know.'

'True. I had a pal who went out with a bus clippy for a month before he found out she was a he.'

'How awful.' She returned with my drink, coming up very close to me as she put it on the counter. She was a temptation I could no longer resist. Her slender waist and the curve of her buttocks beneath that little silky dress, her long, sexy legs and the drift of her perfume finally snapped my elastic and I took hold of her round the waist and drew her between my parted knees.

'Hey . . . what d'you think you're doing?' she asked, knowing damn well. The protest was half-hearted, because while she was making it her hands were coming up to catch hold of my head, to raise my face to look down into and smile upon.

'Only this,' I said hugging her round the hips, her breasts almost touching my nose.

'Why?'

I placed a kiss between her breasts then laid my cheek against them. 'Because it's damn nice, that's why . . . soft and warm and feminine and your perfume's blowing my brains out and if you don't get away from here this instant I shall . . .'

'You shall what?'

I looked up at her. 'I shall kiss the heck out of you.'

With a smile she came down and placed a full-blooded beauty on my mouth, then quickly sprang away and went to attend to the steaks.

'How do you like it?' she asked over her shoulder.

'Pardon?'

She laughed, gave a tut and shook her head. 'Men! Is that all you think about?'

'Mostly. And it's all your fault – women like you. If you all looked like Mrs Carlotti, we wouldn't think of it at all.'

'And what is it about women like me that plunges men's minds below their navels?'

I slipped off the stool and slid up behind her, putting my hands round her waist. 'As if you didn't know.'

'Hey . . . I'm cooking,' she protested, at the same time putting her hands over mine to make sure I didn't leave. 'I *don't* know, you'll have to tell me.'

'All right . . . Well, to start with there's your hair . . . soft, shining, blonde . . . that in itself is enough to get a bloke going. Then, as we work our way south, we come to an ear . . .' I tickled it with my lips and she giggled.

'Stop that!'

'. . . and a neck . . .'

'Stop it!'

'You want to know . . . and two beautiful grey/green eyes . . . a cute and lovely nose . . . and a *fabulous* mouth.'

I pecked her at the corner of her lips and she gave a

little groan and turned her head away. 'Aw, don't do that . . . please,' she mewed, playing games.

'Why not?'

'Never you mind. Go and sit down or I'll burn the steaks . . . and you didn't tell me how you wanted it . . .' she sighed exasperatedly, '. . . your steak!'

'Medium rare,' I laughed. 'But I haven't finished telling you yet.'

'Then you'll have to leave it,' she insisted, 'the steaks are ready. Get some knives and forks out of that drawer . . . and open that bottle of wine.'

'Yes, ma'am.'

We sat opposite each other across the bar counter, sex play temporarily abandoned in favour of general chat, which was more conducive to eating, though it fooled nobody.

'How's your steak?' she asked.

'Marry me – need I say more? It's fantastic. You'll make someone a good wife one day.'

She fluttered her eyelids. 'Oh, do you think so, Russell?'

'Ever been tempted to try it again, Kate?'

She shook her head, then shrugged. 'Oh, now and again I get an urge for permanency . . . but what the hell, the first try wasn't permanent. Signing the paper is no guarantee. No, I guess the answer is no. This is distinctly more fun.'

I smiled at her. 'Yes, it is. I'm *awfully* glad the Fates directed my footsteps . . . well, car tyres . . . towards the *Red Dog* this evening.'

'Me, too. I wasn't going to bother. In fact I'd driven past it then changed my mind. I couldn't face being alone up here, I needed people, strange faces.'

'And you found mine . . . and they don't come much stranger.'

She sipped her wine. 'It's a lovely face – just what the doctor would have ordered for my miserable condition. I was feeling pre-tty lousy.'

'Better now?'

'Much – at least for tonight. Tomorrow I'll have to start

looking for another job . . . or maybe I'll just take a few days off. I've been paid in lieu of holidays. Yes, I might just do that.'

'Where will you go?'

She gave a shrug. 'Who knows? Maybe I'll just point the car south and see where it takes me.'

'What a splendid idea. And I,' I sighed, 'really *will* have to find a new job. I'm bound to get the sack.'

She shook her head. 'No, you won't, it wasn't your fault. You'll live to fight again, I'm sure. Come on, I'll make some coffee; go and put some music on.'

It was around midnight when, as I was about to choose another cassette, she came up behind me and beat me to it. I didn't know what she'd put on until the lazy beat and dreamy drone of Charles Aznavour popped out with 'Dance . . . In The Old Fashioned Way'. And by then her arms were round my neck and we were doing it.

Wonderful record for a nice, slow smooch around the room, her cheek against yours, the perfume of her hair in your nostrils and the press of her warm body against your own.

'Sing it to me, Charlie,' I croaked in her ear. 'Let me stay in your a-a-a-arms . . . Boy, this beats dancing all ends up. Did anyone ever tell you you feel damn good at close quarters, Miss Reinhardt? Tell you something, though, this silky dress material is definitely *not* conducive to Boy Scout behaviour.'

'Good,' she murmured, and snuggled into me even snugger, the grinding undulation of her thighs and belly making mockery of my efforts at self-control.

A moment later and all hope was lost. Reveille had sounded and Herc, like the old soldier he was, rose dutifully to its call.

With comical deliberation, Kate gradually peeled herself away from me, cocked a censurious brow and speared me with one glazed eye. 'And *what* d'you think you're doing?'

'It's not my fault. It's your fault . . . yours and that dress's. I warned you!'

For a moment she held me in a comical dead-pan gaze, then, with a grin, she came in with a rush and plastered herself against me, pressed her belly hard into the old Iron Duke and uttered a gasp of what I hoped was delight, not injury.

'Ohhhhh . . .' she groaned in my ear, her fingers raking furrows in my neck. Now her face came up, asking to be kissed, and I fell into the hot, wet turmoil of her mouth. By heaven, she was hungry. I thought my lips were going to burst.

She broke away, panting, glassy-eyed. 'Russ?'

'Yes, love?' I croaked.

Now she moved away, heading for the door. 'Put the lights out . . .'

I heard the shower running, then stop, heard the bathroom door open and the patter of bare feet padding into the bedroom, and the thought of her walking round stark naked stirred me.

I nipped into the bathroom, flung off my clothes, stepped under the shower, and came out feeling a new man.

She was lying in bed, on her back, covered by a single sheet, every nuance of her body evident in the gentle light that filtered in from the hall.

'You look like an Egyptian mummy,' I grinned from the doorway.

She turned her head and looked at me, slowly, from head to toe, then flicked back the sheet. 'Then come in here and make like an Egyptian daddy.'

I slid in beside her, the touch of her naked body engulfing me with sweet sensation. I kissed her lips, found them ready, willing, gluttonous, then moved down and took her rock-hard nipple in my mouth.

She uttered a groan, moved surgingly against me, her legs splaying wide, yearning for my touch.

At the first, fleeting contact she jerked in spasm and gasped aloud, 'Oh! Oh, *God* that's beautiful . . .'

For a moment or two she became quiet, hung suspended,

as though waiting, listening, momentarily expecting; then, as an express train will suddenly roar out of a quiet tunnel, the orgasm was upon her.

'OHHHHH! . . .' she yelled, a cry of shock, of devastating ecstasy. '*OHHH* . . . my God . . .'

Her arms whipped around me and hugged me almost with desperation as she jerked and jerked against my hand, finally slowing and falling back against the pillow with a deep, replete sigh.

I laughed at her. 'Sounds as though you needed that.'

In answer, she reached for me and hugged me tight, pulled me over her, opened her legs wide and brought me into their moist embrace.

'I want you,' she whispered urgently. 'I want you *inside* me.'

I entered her slowly, inch by throbbing inch, grinning down at her as her eyes grew wider and wider with mock shock.

'My God!' she gasped. 'How much more!'

'Shall I stop?'

'Don't you dare! Oh, Russ . . . oh, that is sen*sati*onal.'

'It's pretty good from up here, too.'

'Tell me something . . .'

'Hm?'

'Are you expected home tonight?'

'Nope.'

'Can you stay?'

'Yep.'

'*Will* you stay?'

I kissed her on the nose. 'Of course I will.'

She gave a delicious squirm, squeezing me. 'You mean . . . I've got your friend all to myself *all* night?'

'If it's okay with him, it's terrific with me.'

'Wow . . .' she chuckled, and began to move against me. '*Oh*, boy . . . Russ?'

'Yes, love?'

'If I . . . should happen to fall asleep . . . *please* wake me up. I couldn't bear the thought of him going to waste.'

'Yes, love.'

'Ohhhh, baby . . .'

'Yes, love?'

She shook her head. 'Nothing. I wasn't speaking to you. I'll see *you* tomorrow morning.

CHAPTER NINE

The buzzing of my watch alarm dragged me up from sleep so deep I must have been close to death. And no flaming wonder. She was still lying on me, where she'd collapsed after her last – and umpteenth – climax, which, according to my reckoning, could have taken place no more than ten minutes ago. And it was now six-thirty!

She stirred and moaned, protesting at the buzzing, and cuddled into me, a mound of warm, delicious flesh, and so help me, the feel of her got me going again, despite the bashing I'd taken over the past six hours.

'Honey . . .' I whispered, giving her a shake. 'It's half past six I must go.'

'Mmmuunnyyuunnggmmmnnns,' she replied, burying her head in my shoulder.

'Baby . . . oops-a-daisy . . .' I slid her gently on to her pillow and again shook her shoulder. 'Kate, angel . . . I must go . . .'

She wasn't having any; she was dead to the world.

I got off the bed and looked down at her, filled my eyes with her sleeping, naked beauty, with the tumble of her hair across the pillow, the faint serene smile on her sexy mouth, and the lines and planes of her beautiful body, then, with a smile, I drew the sheet over her and went into the bathroom.

When I returned, dressed, she was still asleep but was now lying on her back, legs wide apart in an attitude of exhausted abandon.

I sat on the edge of the bed and shook her. 'Honey . . . Kate . . . wake up, baby . . .'

She stirred, groaned, turned towards me and flopped a hand on my knee. 'Mmmmmm?'

'Hey, it's me . . . wake up.'

She propped herself on an elbow and peered at me through a curtain of hair, swaying with sleep. 'What's . . . happening?'

I laughed. 'Nothing . . . but I have to go. It's nearly seven o'clock. I have to get the van back or they'll be sending the cops after me.'

'Oh . . .' she croaked, then, as if suddenly realizing what I was doing, she slipped an arm around my neck and brought me down to the pillow. 'Russ . . .' she kissed me, '. . . don't go. Take those silly clothes off and come back in bed.'

'Aw, baby, don't . . . it's been a terrible fight as it is. You've no *idea* how hard it was for me to get *out* of bed . . . with you lying there all warm and naked and scrummy and . . .' I gulped, '. . . honey, I'll have to go.'

She nodded. 'I know, dammit.'

'Will you take off somewhere today?'

'I think so, just for a few days. Can I reach you when I get back?'

'You bet. It's in the book under Carlotti . . . Balham Grove.'

She kissed me. 'I'll call you. Hey . . .'

'Hm?'

'Thank you for saving my life.'

'And I thank you. I'm ready to tackle the world now.'

'Good.' She blew me a kiss. 'Bye, baby . . . see you soon.'

It was almost seven-thirty when I reached the house, the busiest time possible. Cautiously I opened the front door and peered in. The hall was deserted, though I could hear the family in the kitchen.

I crept in, reached the stairs undetected, and started up them . . . and on the second landing ran straight into Dennis who was coming out of his room.

'Russ!' he gasped. 'What happened to you! I was worried sick . . . thought you'd had a pile-up or something.'

'No, nothing like that, Dennis. I . . . met an old pal, had a few jars too many and stayed the night. Sorry I didn't let you know.'

'That's okay, as long as you're all right. I was dying to hear how you got on yesterday. Sandra told me you were out selling. How did you do? Three-out-of-three, I'll bet.'

I sighed dejectedly, stone-cold reality now banishing the comforting fantasy of the evening. 'Yes, three-out-of-three . . . failures.'

His chin dropped. 'You're kidding.'

'Yes. Come to think of it, they were not failures, they were disasters. So much so that I believe I'm going to get the sack this morning.'

Now his eyes popped. 'What *happened*?'

I glanced at my watch. 'You're going to be late, you'd better get breakfast.'

'Screw breakfast, I want to hear what happened.'

'Okay, come upstairs, I'll tell you while I get shaved.'

He sat on the bed. I got out my electric razor and began to scrape.

'Question One,' I said, 'when you draw appliances from the Stores, are they supposed to be checked?'

He frowned at me. 'Well, sure they are. Doing ten calls a day, we haven't got time to inspect every appliance. That's Ted Faulter's job.'

I nodded. 'That's what I figured. As you know, Polkoski gave me three leads yesterday – a kettle, a food-mixer and a vacuum cleaner. I did the kettle first. I had to climb five flight of stairs to the apartment, and when I got up there and opened the carton . . . there was no flex in it.'

He gaped at me. 'No lead? But that's impossible!'

'Yes, isn't it.'

'Hell, what did you do, Russ?'

'I went down for the flex in the Super De Luxe box . . .'

'That was smart.'

'And discovered there was no plug on the end of it.'

He frowned, deeply mystified. 'No *plug*? Ted Faulter gave you an appliance without a plug on it? Man, that's worse than treason at Zip – Polkoski will go spare if he finds out.'

'Oh, he's going to find out, all right. That little cunt Faulter is going to be hanging by his balls from the rafters by ten o'clock, believe me. I reckon he slipped me *three* Mickey Finns yesterday, not just one, Dennis.'

He was still gaping at me from the first revelation but somehow managed to squeeze a bit more surprise into it. 'Three? You mean he deliberately . . .'

'Yes, I mean deliberately. I had a run-in with him as soon as I met him. Unwittingly I committed the cardinal sin of venturing beyond the counter and into the Stores and he came at me like an enraged bull, quite hysterical. So I gave him a mouthful. I reckon he put the boot in out of sheer malice.'

'I can't believe it! I mean, I know he's a bad-tempered old sod, we're always having a go at him, but I didn't think he'd go to those lengths. What else went wrong?'

'Ha! What didn't! The business about the flex killed the kettle sale stone dead, of course. You don't sell kettles by sticking bare wires into a wall-socket. Made me appear so amateurish she completely lost faith in Zip and virtually threw me out.'

'Oh, blimey . . .'

'Anyway, I spent some of the money you lent me and bought four 13-amp plugs for the rest of the appliances and stuck them on. I thought I'd be okay from there on . . .'

'But?'

'The next call was a food mixer . . . enchanting residence in Bermondsey, down by the docks. Woman with ten kids. She decided to make a couple of cakes there and then to try out the machine . . .'

He shut his eyes in horror. 'What happened?'

'The fucking thing blew up . . . well, almost. Jumped right off the bloody table on to the floor . . . finished up in a million pieces. It simply couldn't take the strain.'

'No!'

'Swear to God, Dennis, I've got the pieces in the van. And she *did* throw me out – after charging me a quid for the food I'd ruined.'

'You reckon the mixer was duff, Russ?'

'I don't know, she did throw an awful lot of stuff into the bowl, but, hell, surely they're made to take it?'

'Well I've never heard of it happening before. And what happened with the vacuum cleaner?'

'Oh, brother . . . the Mark One definitely *was* duff. No suction at all! I tell you, Dennis, that Ted Faulter really stuck it on me. Three out of three is too many for coincidence.'

'Damn right. Well, I'd tell Polkoski as soon as you get in this morning.'

'I intend to. I only hope a certain Mrs Diamond hasn't got to him first.'

'Mrs Diamond? Who's she?'

I grinned. 'A lady who's about to sue Zip out of existence.'

'Eh?'

'It was the vacuum cleaner call. I caused about ten thousand quidsworth of damage in the house.'

'You . . . *what*!'

I switched off the razor, took a clean shirt out of the drawer. 'Never let it be said, Dennis, that Tobin does not make an impression on his clients. "Impact" is the name of the game, and yesterday I made it – in spades. Come on, let's nip over to Kennington and get the sack.'

As we crossed the floor of the warehouse, we encountered Sandra Keane coming out of Polkoski's office, and I knew the game was up by the look on her face. She was wearing the sort of expression one reserves for the sudden and unexpected revelation of a national disaster – like the sinking of the unsinkable Titanic or the outbreak of World War Three.

'Ooo-er,' she exclaimed, staring at me. 'What have you been up to? Mr Polkoski wants to see you right away.'

I turned to Dennis. 'Well, that's it, old chum . . . thanks for the help, sorry I've let you down. I'll let you know visiting hours at Wandsworth. Maybe you can pop in with some snout and a cake with a file in it.'

Despite his concern, he had to laugh. 'Hell, he can't fire you, it wasn't your fault. Ted Faulter's the one who should get the boot.'

'Well, we'll see. Hang on, this won't take long. Perhaps you'd be good enough to drop me off Waterloo Bridge if you're going that way.'

He frowned. 'You mean off *at* Waterloo Bridge.'

'No, I mean "off" Waterloo Bridge.'

I gave him a wink and entered Polkoski's office. The boss was busy sorting out leads for the day. As I entered he looked up, grunted, 'Oh . . . it's you,' then carried on sorting. Several long, twitchy moments passed before he finally, with a burdensome sigh, said, 'I've had phone calls about you . . . from a Mrs Barry and a Mrs Diamond.'

'Oh.'

'At first I was a little confused . . . I thought I was listening to the latest episode of "Some Mothers Do 'Ave 'Em". I doubt if Hitler at the height of his power could've created more havoc in one afternoon than you did.'

'Mr Polkoski, there's an explanation . . .'

He nodded. 'I know there is.' He picked up several leads that he'd placed on one side and held them out to me. 'Here . . . six of the best, let's see what you can do with these.'

I stared at them, at him.

'Well,' he said, 'what're you waiting for?'

'Nothing,' I laughed, taking the leads. 'Thanks, Mr Polkoski.'

'Send in Hopper on your way out.'

Dennis was waiting with bated breath. 'Well?'

I shrugged. 'Beats me. He didn't say a dicky bird, just gave me six more leads! He seemed to know all about it.'

'Well, I'll be . . .'

'Yeh, me, too. He wants to see you.'

'Sure,' he nodded, walking backwards towards the office door, still bemused. 'See you tonight at home!'

'That's a promise.'

Unable to believe Polkoski had taken it so lightly, I crossed the warehouse to Goods Outward, the relief of my escape dissipating with the prospect of facing Ted Faulter again. Steeling myself for the encounter, I pushed through the door and entered the reception area, once again finding it deserted. Now, you little bastard, where are you?

'Anybody there!' I shouted.

I heard sounds of movement among the piles of appliances, now a shuffle of approaching feet along an aisle. Any second now, Faulter, you are going to get yours. By *God*, you're going to get it. And here he . . . came!

A cherubic, ruddy-cheeked face topped by a mop of snow-white hair popped out from a stack of vacuum cleaners and peered at me over John Lennon glasses. He looked like an aged gnome who'd just walked in out of the garden and was looking for his fishing rod.

'Mornin',' he said cheerily, walking towards me. 'What can I do for you?'

I put the six leads on the counter. 'Where's Ted Faulter?'

'Ah, yes, well, he's gorn, hasn't he.'

'Gorn? Gone? You mean he's left?'

He gave a sniff. 'Left is right. Don't know what came over 'im yesterday, they reckon 'e must've 'ad a nervous breakdown or somethin'. 'E went stormin' into Polkoski's office about half-past three an' was never seen again. Next thing, Polkoski came over an' told me I was in charge of Stores! My name's Ben Wallett, by the way, I'm one . . . *was* one of the service mechanics.'

I shook his hand. 'Russ Tobin. I'm a new salesman. And I'm mighty glad you've taken over, Ben. I had a bit of a do with Faulter yesterday, and I reckon he supplied me with duff appliances in spite.'

His brow shot up. 'You were the one!'

'Hm . . . You knew about it?'

'I knew Faulter took three appliances that were waiting for service yesterday afternoon. They were in a stack outside the Service Department. I asked him what 'e wanted them for and all 'e said was, "you'll get 'em back tomorrow." '

I nodded. 'He was right – they're outside in my van. There's a kettle that has no flex, a vacuum cleaner that won't suck, and a food-mixer you'll have to glue together. Well, at least it's a relief to know they *were* duff, but they certainly caused me a bundle of grief yesterday afternoon. The bloody fool, fancy pulling a trick like that. I reckon you're right, he *must* have flipped.'

'It's been coming for a long time, he was getting more and more irritable with the job. Perhaps you were the straw that broke the camel's whatsit. Well, never mind, he's gorn and I'm here now, so let's get you fixed up with some decent appliances. What is it you want?'

I gave him the six leads and off he went, returning in a few minutes with a trolley.

'Here y'are, take these out to the van, then you can bring the duff ones back to me.'

'The service is a bit different from yesterday,' I grinned. 'I hope Polkoski keeps you in this job, Ben.'

'So do I, chum, it's a darned sight easier than the Service Department. Well, off you go then, and see if you can't make up for yesterday.'

'Oh, I intend to. Keep the shop open, I might be back for more this afternoon.'

I wasn't kidding, either. Tobin was about to earn himself some money!

CHAPTER TEN

Funny how life can suddenly change for the better, isn't it? You go through a patch when every damn thing you touch falls apart at the seams, turns to instant disaster, then, as if the Bloke In Charge upstairs says to himself, 'the poor bugger's had enough aggro, we'll give him a bit of luck for a change,' everything begins to come right for a minute or two.

That second day at Zip I couldn't put a foot wrong. The first call I made I sold a Super kettle to a woman in Dulwich without even taking it out of the carton; she was in a hurry and didn't have time for a dem. It was a great start.

The second call was in Brixton, a coloured woman. I showed her the Mark One food mixer and, so help me, she said it looked too cheap – asked me if I had anything better! I brought in the Super and she fell for it hook, line and liquidizer – *and* paid me cash with a thick wad of fivers. No wonder – she had five sons and a husband all working. I reckon they must have been bringing home five hundred quid a week, and good luck to them.

The third call, in Stockwell, was only a toaster but she bought the automatic pop-up Super model as a present for her daughter. The fourth call was out, no reply, but a neighbour told me the old girl would be home at five, so I said I'd call back.

In the afternoon, my fifth call, in Battersea, was tougher. I sweated for an hour demming the Super vacuum cleaner to a fussy little woman who made me clean half the damn house before she finally said she'd take it—but only if I'd give her a year's supply of paper dust-bags. Naturally I agreed and hoped Polkoski would go for the deal.

My last call more than made up for the sweat. I not only

flogged a Super steam iron to a young bird in Wandsworth, but also took an order for one from her pal who had popped in for a cuppa and a chinwag. This is the sort of thing that makes a saleman's life worth living.

After that, I doubled back and did the old girl who'd been out and finished the day with another easy sale of a Super kettle.

Well there's no need to tell you what sort of mood I was in as I drove back to Balham. I felt as if I'd won the pools. Not only had I restored my faith in Tobin's selling ability, but I'd earned a nice fat thirty quid in commission which meant I was already out of debt and back in the black – with the rest of the week to go!

Boy, if I could only keep this up . . . thirty quid a day, six days a week. On a hundred and eighty pounds a week I'd be out of that grotty little attic and into a decent bachelor flat within the month. Not that I didn't appreciate it as a badly-needed roof over the noggin, but it certainly wasn't my intention to stay there for all time. I mean, considerations of personal comfort aside, who knew what was likely to turn up in the romance stakes that would require a bit of unthreatened privacy? Kate, for instance. And/or somebody else, for instance!

Still, that would all take care of itself in due course. The main thing now was to keep selling, selling, selling, and I determined there and then that I'd really get stuck in. What I needed was a target to aim at – say a thousand pounds. Yes, a thousand had a nice ring to it. I'd go like the clappers until I had a thousand in the bank, and then . . . well, who knew? I might quit Zip and try something else, or I might go on and earn another thousand. I'd make the decision when the time came.

Well, for the rest of that week my luck continued to hold, though not every day was as fruitful as the glorious Tuesday.

Wednesday started off with a bang – my van blew up. No, I sold a Super vacuum cleaner before nine o'clock and I thought I was in for another grand clean-up (no pun intended). But it all fell to pieces, the next two clients being out. I recouped a bit in the afternoon with a Super food mixer and two kettles but it wasn't as good as I'd hoped.

Thursday started off slowly but picked up handsomely after lunch, the last call of the day yielding an unexpected Super vacuum cleaner when all the woman had sent in for was a set of electric hair curlers!

And then we come to Friday. Now, Friday you are not going to believe. As I recall what happened that day even *I* have trouble believing it, so you've got no chance. Anyway, believe it or not, here it is.

As soon as I woke up I might have guessed Friday was going to be different, because for one thing the weather had changed. No, I don't mean changed, I mean it had gone berserk, haywire, loopy, as only British weather can when it puts its mind to it.

I flung back the curtains expecting, as usual, to be dazzled by a canopy of brilliant blue sky but was greeted by an overhang of such dense and dirty grey that for a moment I wasn't sure I *had* opened the curtains.

Boy, the rain was coming down in torrents, bucketing down, falling in a sheet so solid I couldn't even see our garden.

'Farewell summer,' I sighed. That was it now till next year – and it was only June!

But my depression was short-lived. I had work to do and the prospect of another bumper day quickly got me going. And down in the dining room even Frank Harris' latest inanity could not quench my good humour.

'Pass the sugar, please, Frank,' I requested.

'Certainly, old boy, certainly . . .'

He placed the bowl in front of me. I dug out a spoonful for my coffee and as I brought it towards me the spoon collapsed on a swinging hinge and the sugar went all over my eggs and bacon.

'HAAAA!' he roared with laughter, thumping the table. 'He fell for it!'

'Ve-ry funny.'

'Oh, for God*sake*!' tutted Julian Frost, tossing his mane

like a lion with a bee in its ear. 'I really don't think that's funny at all.'

'Yers, well, you wouldn't, would you, sweety – because you've got no sense of humour.'

'Tricks like that don't require a sense of humour,' huffed Julian. 'They require psychiatric treatment.'

'Ho, very droll,' scoffed Harris, stuffiing egg into his mouth. 'How's the acting lark coming along, Julian? Any chance of you actually doing any work, is there, God forbid?'

'Acting is *not* a lark, it's a very serious profession,' miffed Julian, inspecting his fingernails. 'But it so happens the theatre is in the doldrums these days.'

'Yeh . . . an' I know who put it there – layabouts like you who call themselves actors. Why don't you jack it in and get a decent job like all of us instead of living off Security which *we* have to pay for?'

'And why don't *you* mind your own sodding business?' seethed Julian. 'One of these days someone's going to give you a bit of your own back, Frank Harris.'

'Ha ha, someone like you, maybe, dear?'

'Yes, someone like me!' retorted Julian, sweeping from the room in high pique.

'Coo, regular little tornado, ain't he?' mocked Harris, helping himself to more toast. 'I know what he needs. Yeh, come to think of it, I've got just the thing for him, too. Watch out for fireworks tomorrow morning, lads, you'll have the laugh of a lifetime.'

I glanced at Dennis; he at me. We weren't going to let it happen.

I looked at my watch. 'We must go, Dennis.'

'Yes, mate.'

We stood at the front door, watching the rain bouncing off the pavement, getting set for a dash to our cars.

'We really will have to do something about Harris,' he said to me fastening the top button of his raincoat.

I grinned. 'I reckon something's being done right now, Dennis.'

'Hm?'

I nodded across the street. There, crouching by the rear near-side wheel of Harris' car, his head and shoulders covered by an old army cape, was the furtive figure of Julian Frost and, as we watched, we could see the car sink lower and lower as the air rushed out of the tyre.

'This I've got to see,' chuckled Dennis. 'He'll be out in a minute. Come on . . .'

We ran to our cars and got in. By the time I'd started the van and cleared the steam from the windows, Julian Frost had disappeared and Frank Harris was crossing the road to his car. He got in, started the engine, put it in gear and drove away from the curb, the realization that both near-side tyres were flat not hitting him until he was in the centre of the road.

Suddenly he braked to a halt, leapt out into the sheeting rain, ran round the car and stood staring apoplectically at the deflated tyres. Then Dennis and I started off.

'Bye, Frank!' I shouted. 'Have a good day, now . . .'

'Hey, TOBIN!' he bellowed, waving me to stop. 'Hey, come back here! HOPPER!'

'Toodle-oo, Frank!' shouted Dennis, driving past him. 'Keep smiling!'

The last view I had of Harris, dumbstruck, standing there with rain cascading off his head like he was standing under a shower, and of Julian, standing in the doorway of the house, killing himself laughing.

Well, at least the day had started off well. How, I wondered, would it continue?

Not in my wildest flights of fancy could I have predicted the outcome of this one!

I had seven leads for the day, one of them for an appliance I hadn't yet handled – an 8mm film projector. This one, sent in by a Mrs Greta Gotlieb, of Roehampton, had special instructions attached not to call before six o'clock in the evening. Obviously wants her husband to inspect the goods, I thought, and tucked her lead away for the end of the day.

I sorted the other six leads out in geographical order, drew my appliances and started off.

The first call was a snip, a kettle in Camberwell. The woman was Australian and not only bought the Super from me but insisted on making me a cup of tea with it and nattering about Sydney for half an hour. Nice soul but talked like a machine gun and I fell out of there quite exhausted.

The next call was a sewing machine in New Cross and I was looking forward to this with particular pleasure, being so confident about the appliance. The customer was a bit of a surprise, though – a Mr Reginald Gilpin. Not often you get men buying sewing machines.

Anyway, with the help of my A.1. Atlas I finally tracked down the address and pulled up outside an enormous old house which, according to the coupon, was obviously divided into apartments, because the address said Flat 6.

I lugged the Mark One machine out of the van and tottered up the driveway, climbed half a dozen stone steps and found the front door ajar, so I went in.

The hallway was dark and smelly. To my right was a door with a number 1 on it; to my left a door with no number at all. And ahead of me rose a wide staircase of well-worn, bare wood treads that looked as though the Roman army had used them in 55BC.

I started up them, my footsteps echoing eerily through the cavernous house, and the higher I got, the darker it got. Gawd, what a place. Could anyone actually *live* here? Even on a bright, sunny day it must have been a bloody depressing house, but today, with the rain lashing down and black clouds riding the chimney pots, it was something out of a Hammer horror movie.

I clomped along the carpetless landing and encountered two more doors, one with a plastic number 3 on it, the second with a painted number 4. Well, at least I was on the right track. Pausing for breath, I started up the next flight of stairs, now wishing Mr Reginald Gilpin had ordered a toaster. It is a well-known fact among sewing machine salesmen that the weight of a machine increases in direct proportion to the number of stairs you have to climb by a factor of one pound to every three stairs, which by now meant I was lugging the equivalent of a baby elephant up this bleeding lot.

Up . . . and up . . . and up . . . I staggered to the top landing, and there dropped the machine and went into a little coma. Ohh, the agony of it. I hung over the bannisters and hee-hawed like a pair of busted bellows. Oh, baby, baby . . . wow . . . whew . . . ohh, that was better.

I sucked in a last big one and turned to look for flat number six.

Problem.

Neither of the doors had a number on it.

Silly buggers.

Well, let's try this one. I knocked.

Now this is where the story gets a *leetle* unbelievable.

The door opened and a girl's face appeared.Quite a nice face but almost lost in a waterfall of crinkly auburn hair, I mean a huge *explosion* of hair. The arty type, I thought, she looks like a mad sculptress.

'Good morning,' I smiled, 'I . . .'

'Ah!' she exclaimed, her eyes going to the sewing machine case. 'I know who you are, do come in.'

'Thank you.'

I stepped into a very long hall that went on forever.

'Beastly day,' she said, shutting the door behind me. 'Come this way, he won't keep you waiting long.'

'Oh, fine . . .'

She came from behind me and led off down the hall, for the first time appearing to me full-length. I bloody-near dropped the machine. She was wearing a dress . . . well, more of a shift thing . . . that was so sheer I could see right through it, and under it she was stark naked! Swear to God! I could see her buttocks, plain as . . . plain as buttocks!

I went hot, then cold, then dizzy. I mean you would, wouldn't you? It's the last thing you expect at ten o'clock on a rainy Friday morning in New Cross.

But this was not all! Suddenly she stopped at a door in

the corridor and turned to *face* me, gave me a bit of a smile and said, 'Would you mind waiting in here? I'll tell him you've come.'

'Er . . .' I didn't know where to put my eyes. It was all there – staring me in the face! Two lovely melons and a big handful of ginger pubes. And she wasn't blinking an eye! 'Yes, certainly,' I croaked.

I walked past her and went into the room, thinking my blood would burst through my veins, the way it was pumping. What was going on here?

I sat down on a wooden chair by a window and tried to figure out what kind of place I'd walked into. It was weird, the whole place was weird, not like an apartment at all. It had an awful *bare* feeling to it. The room I was sitting in was bare, hardly any furniture, just half a dozen cheap wooden chairs.

Just then the doorbell rang and the same bird walked past my open door to answer it. Then the hall was full of people. They began drifting past the door, young guys and gals dressed in jeans and sweaters, ponchos, a raincoat or two. There must have been twenty of them. Finally the red-head walked past and the parade ended.

They must all have assembled in another room just down the hall because I could hear the hubbub of chatter and laughter. Then they quietened and a man's voice took over, talking in low, authoritative tones I couldn't distinguish.

Now he finished speaking and there was a general bustle of activity, followed by a short quiet period, then more activity, and that moment the red-head appeared in the doorway.

'Would you come through now, please?'

Utterly baffled, I picked up the machine and followed her down the hall and into a huge room on the right . . . and came to a stunned halt in the doorway. Believe me or believe me not, I tell you the gospel truth.

The room was full of naked people!

So help me, all those kids who had just arrived were standing around chatting, as bare-assed as the day they were born. I just stood there pole-axed, didn't know what to do or where to look, because everywhere I settled my eyes were bums and tits and pubes and dangling dicks and . . .

Out of the *mêlée* came a middle-aged bloke dressed, thank God, in shirt and slacks. He advanced on me with a smile, a crumpled, dissolute-looking individual with sparse blond hair and effeminate hands.

'Yes,' he said, taking me by the arm and leading me into the naked throng, 'now, we'll do a cursory run-through for you to give you a general idea what we're trying to achieve. Madeleine, darling . . . Karen, Roy and Charles . . . take up your positions over here. Ursula and Jenny . . . over here. The rest of you back against the far wall and come in *slowly* on the count of three . . . all right, everybody ready? And a-one . . . two . . . three . . .'

I stood rooted, as a tableau of theatrical rape enfolded before me – Roy and Charlie wrestling Madeleine and Karen on to the ground, then following them down for a good screwing; Ursula and Jenny apparently waiting in the wings, terrified, for the same treatment, and the rest of the gang advancing with stylised stealth for a good butcher's.

Now the group began to chant, to stamp rhythmically as they neared the pseudo-copulating couples, urging the men on to bigger and better rape. The group encircled them, drew the reluctant Ursula and Jenny into their midst, and proceeded to weave intricate patterns of movement around and between the doodling duos, waving their arms and maintaining the meaningless chant as they snaked in and out, through and around, doubling back on themselves, forming arches and tunnels. Now bursting outwards like the unfolding petals of a flower, now reforming and lifting Ursula and Jenny high into the air in the attitude of sacrifice . . . And while all this was going on I was standing there with my mouth open, eyes bulging, wondering when my alarm clock would go off and wake me from this unbelievable dream.

'You see the problem . . .' a voice murmured in my ear.

It was the blond bloke, standing close behind me. 'As I told you on the phone we can't get into the cellar for another two weeks, we've simply *got* to work out the lighting here. It's going to be difficult for you, I know, but we have no choice.' He looked down at the sewing machine case and gave it a tap with his foot. 'What have you brought with you? I feel very strongly about strobe, I think it could be immensely effective when they're actually fucking, but I'm open to any other suggestion you might have in mind. Can you rig strobe in here?'

'Er . . .'

'I'm frightfully sorry to hit you with this, but Freddy did say if there's one company that could help us out it's Enticing Lighting. Perhaps I'm rushing you. Would you like to *absorb* the scene for a minute or two, get the feel of it. I'll let them run through the entire rape sequence, if you like, and you can just wander around and think it out . . . All right?'

'Er, yes . . . f . . . fine.'

He moved away, his eyes and concentration on the performers. Now was my chance to get out, to escape. All I had to do was pick up my ridiculous sewing machine and walk out. I didn't know who the hell they were or what sort of show they were rehearsing, but I knew I was in the wrong bloody flat and I had to get out before they discovered who I really was and . . .

'Hi, how's it going?' It was the red-head who'd crept up behind me. I turned . . . oh, Jesus, now *she* was bollock naked!

'I . . .' I couldn't speak, my throat was choked, my brain was spinning and my eyes wouldn't focus properly.

She frowned at me. 'Are you feeling all right? You look a bit off.'

'I . . . it's a bit hot in here.'

She gave a grin. 'Take your clothes off like the rest of us . . . or perhaps that's what's making you sweat?'

'Oh, no . . . no, I'm used to . . . this sort of thing.'

'So – take your clothes off.'

'Er . . . well, actually . . . I have to go down to the van

for . . . some equipment. Yes, I want to bring up some strobe lighting.'

'Ah, you've decided to use strobe – good. You want to go down now?'

'Yes . . . right now.' I picked up the machine.

'I'll see you out . . . make sure the door's locked.'

I began to move towards the door of the room, my neck hairs prickling with premonition, anticipating an objection from Blondie at any second, but no objection came.

At last I was out in the hall, out of that room, and heading for the front door.

'Will you want any help?' asked Starkers. 'I'll slip something on and come down with you.'

'Oh, no! No. thanks very much, I can . . . manage. I won't be long.'

'All right . . .'

We reached the front door. Her hand went to the lock catch, she pulled it open to let me through . . . and I almost ran into a young bloke in jeans and seaman's sweater, who had his hand raised to press the bell.

'Oh!' he smiled at me. 'That saved me a job. I'm John Hall from Enticing Lighting, I . . .'

I was past him in two strides. 'See the lady behind the door!'

'Hey!' cried Starkers. 'Hey, come back you! Who are you?'

I hurtled down the stairs at ninety.

Down in the lower hall I encountered an elderly, grey-haired man coming in from the street with a carrier bag of groceries. He held the door open for me, nodded amiably.

'Thank you,' I panted. 'Tell me, do you know a Mr Reginald Gilpin?'

He hesitated suspiciously. 'Gilpin? Yus, top floor, flat 6. But you won't find 'im in this time a day, he'll be round at the pub.'

'Oh. Tell me, which is his flat on the top floor?'

'I told yuh, flat 6.'

'Yes, but there are no numbers on the doors up there. Is his flat the one on the left?'

'Oh, yus, on the left. That's flat 6. The other one's flat 5.'

'And who lives in flat 5?'

'Huh,' he scoffed, 'some crazy theatrical fella . . . name of Jason Mason or Mason Jason or somethin'. I don't know what goes on up there but I'm sure it's not 'olesome. Reggie Gilpin says he's seen girls walkin' around half-naked in that flat when the door's bin open. 'e reckons Mason uses the place to re'earse dirty shows that 'e puts on somewhere.'

'Disgusting,' I tutted. 'Half-naked, hm, that's awful.'

'Er . . . shall I tell Reggie you called? What's it about?'

'Russ Tobin from Zip Electrics. He sent in a coupon for a sewing machine demonstration.'

'A sewing machine?' frowned the old lad. 'What the 'ell's he want a sewing machine for?' He put his hand on my arm. 'Lissen, take no notice of 'im, you're wastin' your time, son. 'E does all sorts of funny things when he's had a skinful. 'E once sent in a coupon for a corset fitting! 'e's not quite all there, is poor old Reggie.'

'Oh . . . well, thanks for the tip. I'll be on my way.'

He opened the door for me and as I went through, a little stout woman came puffing up the steps and called out, 'Yoo hoo, wait for me, Mr Gilpin! I've forgotten my key!'

Gilpin! What the *hell* went on in this crazy house!

I didn't hang around to find out.

CHAPTER ELEVEN

I suppose I never really fully recovered from that shock encounter with all those naked birds. Certainly my mind wasn't fully on my work the rest of the day. I'd be driving along and suddenly find myself totally lost in a vivid day-dream of how it had been, with me right there in the thick of it, surrounded by dancing, prancing, chanting bodies and the four on the floor going at it heavens hard . . . or to be exact heaven's soft, as it was only a dry run, so to speak.

Did that mean, I asked myself, that on the night, those fellas would actually . . . *rape* those girls . . . on a *stage* . . . in front of an *audience*?

Nah, they wouldn't . . . couldn't. Would they? Could they? God knows. Who was to say what lengths they went to these days, if you'll pardon the expression. I'd heard that live sex shows were old hat in Hamburg, so why not in London? Yeh, I guess it was possible.

What would it be like – I wondered – watching a live sex show? I tried to visualize it . . . going to the theatre or whatever, buying a ticket at the box office, asking the bird in the box, 'What time does the last performance start, Miss?'

'It's just started, sir. You'll have to hurry, he's already got it up her.'

'Oh . . . no time to buy some sweets, then?'

'Not if you want to see him finish. He's a bit of a fast merchant, this one. Now, next week we've got Half Hour Harry on the bill, he's my favourite, really takes his time, does Harry . . . oops, sorry sir, you're too late, there goes the bell now, it's all over. Like to book for tomorrow night?'

Ridiculous.

Fascinating, though. So fascinating that the unreality of what I had encountered continued to enshroud me in a strange, though not unpleasant, miasma of unreality for the rest of the day – a state of suspended, dream-like animation in which I was incapable, I knew, of further shock. Which was why, I suppose, I was able to cope so readily with the outrageous developments that took place that evening at Flat 36, New Rochelle Mansions, Roehampton.

Had I encountered the incredible Gerta Gotlieb in a condition of cold, early-morning emotional sobriety, I may well have turned tail and fled the moment she opened the door (though, then again, I may not!). But in my state of stunned preparedness for anything weird, outlandish, abnormal or downright kinky that life was likely to throw my way, I merely took the Gotlieb promise of spectacular adventure in my stride, accepting it as a gift for which Fate had been conditioning me all day.

It was plop on six o'clock when I reached the Mansions, an extremely well-to-do block of modern apartments tucked away from the main Roehampton road behind a high brick wall and private gardens.

The rain had at last stopped, but the sky was an ugly dark mauve, full of rain to come, and the wind was wet and chill. A night to spend in front of an open fire with a bottle of brandy and a good book – if there was nothing more entertaining at hand.

I parked the van in an area marked out for parking at the side of the building, took out the Mark One projector, locked up and walked round to the main entrance. Through double glass doors I entered a palatial, marble-walled lobby where I found the customary row of two-way intercoms set in the wall near the elevators.

I pressed the button of number 36, and had a look round while I waited. All very swish, very expensive. And again I paused to wonder why the Gotliebs, who obviously were not pushed for a bob or two, would bother with a cut-price film projector.

Yours is not to wonder why, Tobin, yours is to get up there and flog your little heart out.

'Hello?' said the speaker grille. My word, she had a lovely voice – as deep and husky as Sandra Keane's plus a *very* sexy foreign accent. German, I suspected.

'Mrs Gotlieb?'

'Yes.'

'My name is Tobin . . . I'm from Zip Electrics. I have a film projector to show you . . .'

'Ah, yes! Please come up to the third floor.'

I punched a button and got an elevator immediately, rode up to the third and walked down an extremely carpeted corridor to flat 36. As I touched the buzzer the door opened.

My word, she was a big lady. Not fat, but big, solid, tall, broad-shouldered, the sort Hitler had in mind for breeding his Super Race.

She was a blue-eyed blonde in her mid-thirties, a good-looking woman though her features were a touch on the heavy side to be called beautiful. Striking, you'd say.

She was wearing a very expensive ankle-length house-coat of oyster velvet trimmed with pale fur that did wonders for her, gave her a frothy femininity, which detracted from her bigness, though even this superbly cut creation could not hide the fact that she was endowed with a pair of knockers a fella could high-dive into and be lost to the world forever.

'Russ Tobin,' I smiled, expecting her to stand back and let me in.

She didn't move. She just looked at me, all of me, up and down and up again, a twinkle of amusement in her eyes, and the old thumper gave a bit of a stumble. I'd met her type before; she was a man-eater.

'How nice,' she purred, arching a cute brow. 'You'd better come in, Russ Tobin.'

I walked past her into a cloud of exotic perfume so sensually potent I thought I was being chloroformed. It was a heavy, fullbodied aroma, evoking thoughts of an Indian temple or a Spanish ballroom in high summer, of pungent tropical flowers in an African garden, of nights of torrid love under a Caribbean moon.

Suddenly I was no longer in Roehampton, England. As she closed the door behind me, she shut off that world completely and transported me into a world of make-believe. I could have been anywhere . . . in a flat in Rome, Paris, Madrid, Rio de Janeiro, and wherever it was, I was very happy to be there. To hell with Roehampton, who needed Roehampton?

She turned from the door and smiled at me, an intimate, friendly smile, putting me at ease. 'Did you get wet? It's been a frightful day.'

'Not wet, just damp.'

'Then come and un-damp and show me what you've brought.'

She went ahead of me, led me down the hall and into a large, stunningly-furnished, split-level living room, its raised section occupied by a gleaming white grand piano, its lower level a lounge of sumptuous comfort – including a crackling log fire in an Adam fireplace!

I followed her down into the lounge, now further removed from Roehampton than ever, revelling in the outrageous luxury of the place and marvelling that a penniless bloke like me could be here to enjoy it.

This, of course, is one of the perks of being a salesman. Granted, most of the places you visit do tend to lean more towards 226 Paradise Road, Bermondsey than Buckingham Palace, but now and again you get to set foot in a lovely place like this and it more than makes up for the grot.

'A magnificent apartment,' I said as we descended into the lounge.

'Thank you. Come and sit here by the fire. Put the machine on that table. You're in no great hurry, are you?'

'Er . . . no . . .'

'Good, then you will have a drink and warm yourself.'

As I sank into the deep cushioning of a turquoise settee, she crossed to an antique cabinet on which a bottle of champagne, in a silver bucket, and glasses were set out on a silver tray. Now I noticed the bottle was opened; she'd already been at it.

As she poured the drinks I had a squint round the place, looking for clues as to what she was, who she was, who her old man might be. There were several framed photographs dotted around: two or three of her, glamorous portraits done by a top class photographer; and one of her and a much older man, a very distinguished cove with grey hair and a million-dollar smile, standing with their arms around each other outside a million-dollar pink villa in the South of France or somewhere.

In another photograph she was standing with the same bloke on the deck of a yacht, both of them in shorts, waving at the camera, looking very tanned and very rich. And yet another photograph was of the yacht under full sail; it was no twelve-foot dinghy.

As she turned from the cabinet with two glasses, her housecoat briefly parted to give me a flash of naked thigh. She looked as though she'd just stepped out of the bath. She set the glasses down on an amber-marble coffee table in front of me, then moved off in another direction to an antique stereogram and hit the button, and as she turned for home, orchestral strings and a soulful piano seeped into the room, completing my undoing.

She sat on the settee, an armslength from me, leaned back into it, closed her eyes and simultaneously crossed her legs, the gown again opening, the close proximity of her bare legs bringing up a lump in my throat the size of a tennis ball. Boom . . . boom . . . boom . . . went the heart, thud . . . thud . . .thud . . . went the blood. Batten down the hatches, son, it's coming down harder.

'How old are you?' she asked softly.

I cleared my throat. 'I'm . . . twenty-six.'

'A beautiful age. Are you married?'

'No, I'm not.'

'I was married at nineteen. I married a duke.'

'Oh, really?'

'Then I married a count.'

'Good heavens . . .'

She laughed. 'Then I married a baron.'

'My word, that's some going.'

She laughed again, opened her eyes and looked at me. 'I like you, you're sweet.' She sat up and reached for a glass, handed it to me, took up her own. 'To the sweet bird of youth.'

We sipped the champers. She relaxed back against the cushions, fondling her glass, smiling into the flickering fire. 'Where do you live?'

'In Balham . . . in a boarding house.'

'Ah, a boarding house. I once lived in a boarding house . . . a very long time ago.'

'Where was that – in Germany?'

She smiled. 'How clever of you . . . yes, in Germany.' She glanced around the lovely room. 'It wasn't at all like this.'

'No, I dare say it wasn't.'

She looked at me. 'You understand. I knew you would.'

She drained her glass and held it out to me, then changed her mind. 'No, bring the bottle over here.'

I got up and went to the cabinet, and when I turned with the tray found her studying me with a soft, dreamy expression. 'You remind me of someone I once knew.'

'Oh?' I put the tray on the table and sat down to refill her glass. 'Who was that?'

She gave a little shrug. 'A boy. Thank you, fill your own, too.' As I topped up my glass I felt her eyes burning into me and had to fight hard to stop the bottle shaking. It was an awful lot of woman sitting there.

'Do you like me?' she asked suddenly, very softly.

My blood erupted. I looked up at her, my brain swimming, overwhelmed by her, by her perfume, status, bigness, by her sexuality. I felt choked, unable to speak.

'Very much,' I managed to croak.

'Good,' she smiled, fingering the lip of her glass. 'Tell me . . . are you a good boy . . . or a naughty boy?'

'I . . . well, I . . .'

Oh, blimey.

'Have you made love to many girls?'

'Er . . . well . . .'

Her smile deepened. 'I know you have. I'll bet you do it very well, too. Do I frighten you?'

I grinned, beginning to steady up a bit. 'No.'

'That's good, I don't want to frighten you . . . I want us to have a nice time together. Are you going anywhere this evening? You have a date with your girl?'

'No, I have no plans to go out. I don't get paid till tomorrow, so I couldn't if I wanted to.'

She frowned at me. 'You are broke? Oh, how awful . . . a young man should not be broke. Does this job not pay very well?'

'Not bad, but I've only been doing it a week. I've just come back from Ireland . . . well, from right round the world, really, and I haven't had a chance to save any money yet.'

She raised a surprised brow. 'From right round the world? That sounds interesting, what were you doing?'

'Oh, this and that . . . I sort of worked my way round.'

'I like that . . . an adventurous spirit. I detected that in you as soon as I saw you.'

'You did?'

'Hm hm,' she nodded. 'I thought to myself here is a young man who likes a bit of fun, a bit of adventure. I saw it in your eyes. You have very naughty eyes, you know.'

I laughed. 'Do I? I didn't know that.'

'Oh, come, you must have been told that before by women. I'm sure you must have left a trail of broken hearts behind you round the world. The eyes do not lie, you know, they are the mirror of the soul. Whatever we think, feel and do shows the world what we are.' She laughed teasingly and stabbed my knee with her finger. 'And I think *you* are a very naughty boy. Don't bother to deny it, I see what I see. Pour me some more champagne.'

Again, as I refilled our glasses, I was conscious of her eyes on me and could almost hear her mind working, feeding in impressions, information, details of progress, in order to determine future course of action, and quickly reaching the conclusion that any damn thing she had in mind was all right by me – which it was.

'I suppose you're wondering,' she said, reaching for her glass, 'why I sent in that coupon for the film projector?'

'Yes, I have been wondering . . . especially now that I've met you.'

'Oh? Why now especially?'

I shrugged. 'It doesn't seem the sort of thing you'd normally do – shop by mail order. I feel you're the kind of woman who likes to go to a shop, inspect the goods, ask for a dozen demonstrations before you buy. Also, I wouldn't have thought a film projector is the sort of thing you would buy, anyway. It's usually a man's job. I expected your husband to be here.'

She smiled wickedly. 'How d'you know he isn't?'

'Hm?'

She laughed aloud. 'How d'you know he isn't here . . . in the bedroom, the bathroom?'

'Well, I don't, of course.'

'No, you don't, do you. I'm teasing you, he's not here . . . nor is he likely to be. And the answer to why I sent in the coupon is simple – I did it on impulse. I opened the newspaper, saw your advert and . . .' She shrugged.

'Do you have any films?'

A secret smile. 'Yes, I have some films.'

'How about a screen?'

She hesitated. 'Yes . . . sort of. I have a wall.'

'Oh. Well, I suppose that would do for a demonstration.' I looked round the room. This wouldn't do at all. Apart from the fact that the wallpaper was a pale green patterned flock, there were too many pictures, mirrors, wall-lights and things to project a film.

'No, not in here,' she said. 'It's another room.'

'Oh, fine. Would you . . . like to see the projector now?'

'Why not?'

I got up, collected the machine and looked at her expectantly, expecting her to make a move to the other room, but she didn't.

'I'd like to see it first,' she said. 'Put it here on the table.'

I opened the box, took out the projector, placed it before her and sat down beside her again, rehearsing its selling points in my mind.

'Well, now, this is the Zip Projector Mark One. It has an ultra sharp 15-25 mm f/1.4 zoom lens . . . a variable speed control . . . and a fast re-wind. For the price it's a very good machine.'

'Mmm . . .' she said doubtfully. 'It doesn't look terribly strong. Is it built to last?'

I smiled. 'Depends on how much you're going to use it, Mrs Gotlieb.'

'That's difficult to say. But I think more important factors are that it should be reliable and easy to use. I'm not very mechanically minded. I want something that virtually runs itself, that's very easy to load – like these new pocket cameras.'

My heart quickened, 'Ah! Then you're talking about the Super De Luxe model.'

'Oh?' she frowned. 'What is that?'

I got to my feet. 'Let me show it to you, I have one in my car. I'm sure it's exactly what you're looking for.'

'All right,' she smiled. 'Go and get it. Slip the lock on the door as you go out.'

'Right.'

Jubilantly, I left the flat and rode down in the elevator, the feeling of unreality, not totally undue to the champagne, now stronger than ever. It was all a dream, a fantasy . . . a fabulous apartment and a wanton, sexy woman all to myself – *and* the likelihood of flogging her a Super projector. It couldn't be true.

Yet here I was, taking the Super out of the van, now heading back to the elevators, riding up to the third floor, walking along the corridor . . .

Something had to go wrong, I told myself, it couldn't be this good. I'd get back and find she's changed her mind, gone off the boil, had suddenly realized what she was doing and come to her senses. She'd be on the phone, talking to her husband who'd changed his plans and was coming home immediately . . . *some*thing would go wrong.

I reached her door, expecting to find it re-locked . . . but no, it was ajar, as I'd left it. I entered the flat, closed and locked the door, and made my way into the living room.

She wasn't there.

'I'm back!' I called out, walking down the steps into the lounge.

Silence.

A ripple of unease pervaded me. This was the *Marie Celeste* all over again . . . a cigarette burning in the ashtray, her glass half-filled with champagne, music playing on the stereogram . . . but *she* had disappeared!

I put the Super down, unpacked it and settled the projector on the coffee table beside the Mark One, suddenly convinced it was all a waste of time. Something *was* wrong! She'd gone, walked out, flown the coop! With growing unease, bordering on jitters, I looked around the room, half expecting to see her crumpled body lying behind an armchair, victim of a burglary and mugging while I'd been gone.

My imagination took off. Was *I* the unwitting victim of some diabolical plot? Had I been lured into this situation as the fall-guy for some dastardly crime that had been committed earlier in another room? Would I hear police sirens any second now and be caught red-handed at the scene of the crime!

Okay, so it was crazy – but a drugstore delivery boy had found himself in precisely this situation in a recent Kojak story . . . or was it Harry O? No, I tell a lie, it was Colombo . . .

'Ah, you're back,' she said, coming into the room from the hall. 'I've been getting things ready.' As she came down the steps, she frowned at me. 'Are you feeling all right, you look a bit . . .'

'Fine,' I grinned. 'It must be the champagne.'

Her eyes went to the projector. 'Ah, now that looks more like it.'

She sat on the settee and inspected it closely, comparing

the two machines. 'What does this one do that that one doesn't?'

I sat beside her. 'A great deal, Mrs Gotlieb. You said you wanted ease of operation, well, this one does practically run itself. You simply load the full reel on the front spindle, feed the end of the film into this guide-way, press this switch, and the machine threads itself automatically. In addition to that, it has reverse and still projection, a much better zoom lens for really big close-ups, ultra-fast re-wind . . . *and* facilities for recording and mixing sound.'

'Sound! My word, that is impressive. And how much is this machine?'

'Well, naturally you'd expect to pay more for a projector of this calibre . . .'

'Oh, naturally,' she smiled, mocking me with her eyes. 'How much more, Mr Tobin?'

'Well, this comes out at . . . a hundred and sixty-four pounds . . . actually.'

'Mmm . . .' she murmured, her eyes twinkling, reflecting her enjoyment of the game she was playing. 'That's a lot of money. And how much would it be worth to you?'

'I make ten percent.'

She pursed her lips. 'Sixteen pounds? I think that deserves a most thorough demonstration, don't you?'

'Oh, yes, of course. I'd want to give you a thorough demonstration anyway. I'd want to make sure you knew how to work the machine before I left you.'

'How very refreshing to meet a dedicated man.' She looked at me, devoured me with her eyes, the smouldering sexiness of her gaze starting up the most awful trembling inside. Her lips parted provocatively and she said softly, 'Bring your lovely machine through to the other room and we'll see what it can do.'

She got up and floated away up the stairs, leaving me to follow.

When I reached the door she'd disappeared again, but there was a light on in a room down the hallway. I went to it . . . finding myself in the doorway of a fabulous Arabian Nights bedroom.

Near the centre of the room, looking as though it had been pulled out from its normal position against a wall, was a vast oval bed, covered with a black satin counterpane, its headboard a curved and intricately-carved, richly-padded affair, designed, with the aid of bolster cushions, to offer the ultimate in lounging comfort. Immediately behind the bed she had placed a tall white pedestal table which probably normally held a potted plant or a vase of flowers, but which now was obviously intended to take the projector. She'd even provided an extension lead which snaked across the thick white carpet from an outlet in the right-hand wall.

To my left, a run of white, ornately filigreed wardrobe cupboards lined the wall, separated into two sections by a wide dressing table unit, above which was a stretch of white-painted wall, some six feet wide by four feet deep, on which she intended to project the film.

As I appeared in the doorway, she turned from the dressing table and held out several canisters of 8 mm film, asking, 'Will this wall be all right?'

'Perfect,' I croaked.

'I had the bed designed for watching TV, it's wonderfully comfy. So I thought why not do the same thing with a film propector? Do you not think it's a good idea?'

'Excellent. Do you have many films, Mrs Gotlieb?'

'A few. But if I like the arrangement I shall buy lots more. So many nights there is so little worth watching on television. I like the idea of controlling my entertainment . . . of being able to pander to a particular mood.'

'Indeed . . . that's what having money is all about, isn't it?'

She smiled.

While I set up the projector, she knelt up on the bed, her arms on the headboard, and watched me.

'Which film would you like first?' I asked her.

She studied the canisters, sorted them out, then put them on the table next to the projector. 'Show them in that order, would you?'

'You're the customer,' I grinned.

'Not yet. It depends on what sort of demonstration you give me.'

'Of course.'

I removed the first reel from its canister and loaded it on to the front spindle, fed the leader into the guide-way, and said, 'Now, all you do is . . .'

I turned on the switch. Smooth as silk the leader ran through the machine and emerged at the rear to be fed into the rear spool.

'Voilà!' I said. 'That's all there is to it. Now it's ready to go.'

'How splendid! I'm sure I could manage that.'

'Are you ready? Shall I put the light out?'

'No – go and get the champagne, we will do this properly.'

'All right,' I grinned. 'You take a seat in the Dress Circle.'

When I returned from the lounge with the tray, she was lying on the bed, propped up against the cushions in a pose of supreme languor, one knee raised, the gown split open almost to her crotch, though she'd covered her legs with the folds of the gown.

I put the tray on the dressing table, topped up our glasses and turned towards her, the trembles starting up again at the sight of her sprawled out on the bed with her legs parted like that.

'Thank you,' she said, taking her glass. 'I must say you'd make a lovely butler. Perhaps I'll offer you the job.'

I grinned twitchily. 'Perhaps I'd take it. Are you ready now?'

'Hm? Oh, for the film! Yes, I'm ready.'

I went behind the bed and turned off the wall-light. Now the room was illuminated only from the glow of light entering from the hallway, enough to see by without being a distraction to the film.

I switched on the projector. The leader threw stark white light at the wall but lasted only a second or two, then the film began.

Immediately I could tell it was a home movie. The scene,

in colour, was a shoreline of a bay, shot at some distance from a boat. Now a closer shot revealed the hotels and villas of a Spanish-type town, a small community running down almost to the water's edge.

The camera panned slowly right, along the shore, taking in the bustle of traffic and beach activity, then slowly tilted up and up and zoomed in on a fabulous pink villa set high up on the edge of a cliff which overlooked both sea and town.

The scene now changed to a closer shot of the villa, taken in the garden, the villa rising above camera, proudly and majestically, surveying what must have been a breath-taking marine view.

The screen blazed with colour, the pale pink of the villa walls contrasting with dazzling displays of tumbling, clinging, spreading flowers in hues of purple, yellow and orange so brilliant they almost hurt the eyes. The glory of a Spanish garden in high summer.

'Fabulous,' I murmured. 'Is it Spain?'

'South of France . . .' she said quietly. 'Near Cannes.'

Oh, well . . .

For the next minute or so the camera dodged about all over the place, shooting the villa from different angles, showing its magnificent gardens, tennis courts, swimming pool complex, and its several panoramic views of distant town, mountains and sea.

I was about to make a crack about it reminding me of home when the lady herself popped on to the screen. She was standing in the garden of the villa, a year or two younger and every stupendous inch of her as brown as a nut, at least the bits that were not covered by a tiny multi-coloured bikini that more closely resembled three foreign stamps than a swimsuit.

By gum, she *was* a big lady.

Laughing, the breeze ruffling her sun-bleached hair, she waved at camera and walked off across the garden, the camera zooming in cheekily on to her swaying bottom.

I looked down at Gerta and found her grinning, remembering the moment.

'Superb garden,' I commented and she laughed.

'That was a fabulous summer . . . three glorious months of sun, sand and sea. I never wanted it to end.'

'Who was the lucky cameraman?'

She glanced up at me, smiling, then back to the screen. 'You'll see in a moment.'

When the answer was revealed it came as no surprise. It was the old boy in the photograph in the lounge.

'Is it the baron?' I asked her and she nodded.

'Yes. This was our honeymoon.'

'Oh. How wonderful. How long ago was it?'

'Three years ago. He's very sweet but a hopeless husband,' she said matter-of-factly. 'He buys wives as other men buy cars. I am his seventh.'

'Oh.'

The film ran out and I put on the wall-light while I rewound. Gerta got off the bed and went to replenish our glasses, saying as she returned, 'I'm awfully glad I have those times on film. When I'm feeling low I will run them and cheer myself up. Sunshine always cheers me up.'

'Me, too, I love it.'

She came up close to put my glass on the table, then, unexpectedly, ran her fingers through my hair. 'I'm sure you do. You look the sunshine type. You'd have loved the villa . . . I would have liked to have you there.'

'Me, too,' I gulped, startled by the intimacy of her gesture.

She smiled at me, a warm, languorous smile, and I could tell she was getting nicely bombed. Then, with a playful prod on my nose with her finger, she turned away and sprawled on the bed, this time giving me an overhead shot of her naked thighs.

'Ready with the next one?' she asked, settling herself into the cushions.

'Yes.'

I put out the light and rolled the projector.

It was more of the same, except it was a different villa in a different location with a different older man. And in this one she looked incredibly young.

'The duke,' she offered, reading my mind.

'You mean you were a real duchess!'

She laughed and waved her glass. 'For one whole month! Mind you, it was of a Central European dukedom nobody had ever heard of! Still, it served its purpose.'

I watched her cavorting on a beach with a beachball, posing against a sunset on a sand dune, a sun-tanned Juno in a golden swimsuit, her golden hair cascading down her back and the proud mound of her breasts jutting in mouth-watering relief against the crimson orb.

'Quite a girl, hm?' she murmured.

'Quite a girl,' I concurred. 'And still quite a girl.'

I saw her smile. 'You think so, Russ Tobin? I was twenty then . . . you'd have thought so then. I'm an old lady now.'

'Ha!' I laughed, knowing she didn't mean a word of it.

The film went on, most of it of Gerta – at the villa, at a picnic, on a motor cruiser, standing at the controls next to a big, broad-shouldered, handsome, dark-haired fellow with flashing eyes and flashing teeth.

'Who is he?' I asked.

'Our chauffeur,' she answered with a smile. 'A beautiful man. He helped save my sanity.'

I'll bet.

'Sounds as though you had a rough time with the duke,' I commented.

'It's a miracle it lasted a month,' she said, almost to herself, and was about to say more but the film finished. This had been a particularly short film, perhaps indicative of their particularly short marriage.

I rewound it and put on the third film, also a short one. This, too, was similar stuff, with Gerta looking a fantastic twenty-five or so. Here, she was posing in the gardens of a huge Gothic house, in what looked like the Bavarian alps, a hellish-looking place of solid grey stone with turrets and a castellated roof and an iron-studded front door built to withstand a siege.

'Cosy,' I remarked. 'The count's *pied-à-terre* I take it?'

She laughed and nodded. 'He doesn't appear, though, he was the shy type.'

'Ah. Who was shooting the film?'

The answer came up on the screen a few seconds later. He was another tall, well-built bucko with flashing eyes and flashing teeth, dressed in a morning suit he looked about to burst out of.

'He,' she answered with a grin.

'Your butler?'

She nodded, still grinning to herself.

'Did he help save your sanity, too?'

She threw back her head and laughed.

'Tell me, who *chose* all these butlers and chauffeurs for you?'

'I believe that is what they call a rhetorical question, isn't it?'

The film came to an end.

While I rewound and reloaded, she knelt up at the bed-head and watched me, her chin on her arms and a big twinkle in her eye, beginning to look beautifully mellow now.

'I have many more films like that, but I wanted you to see those as a sort of introduction . . . to help you to get to know me better, do you know what I mean?'

I certainly did.

'I wanted you to understand . . . to get things into their correct perspective.' She smiled secretively. 'I think you're going to enjoy the next one much more.'

'Oh? What's this one?'

She waggled a finger at me. 'Wait and see. You're not drinking your champagne. Drink it up and I'll get some more.'

I emptied the glass, beginning to float very nicely myself by now. She went to the dressing table, weaving a bit, and returned with brimming glasses, taking a sip from each. I went to take mine from her but she smiled and shook her head. 'No . . . I don't think it's right that you should stand up there while I'm enjoying all this comfort. Take off your shoes and jacket and try my beautiful bed.'

Aye aye . . .

I threw my jacket over a chair, kicked off my shoes, put out the light and started the projector, then climbed on to the bed beside her and sank into the posture moulded cushions. It was like sit-lying on a sumptuous sun-bed.

'Your tie . . .' she said. 'You can't possibly relax in a tie.'

I threw it on the floor. She handed me my drink and raised her glass to me. 'Comfy?'

'Fantastic.'

'Watch the film.'

The opening scene told me this was no home movie. It was an establishing shot of a banquet, set in an ancient Roman palace, attended by about a hundred costumed revellers. The camera commenced a long, slow tracking shot around the tables, which formed three sides of a square, showing us that all the men were young, handsome, virile, and the girls were all beautiful and splendidly endowed.

So far everything looked respectable. There was a lot of laughing and giggling and wine-swilling going on, a bit of grape-feeding and over-the-shoulder bone-chucking, but nothing you wouldn't find at most Hampstead wine-and-cheese parties.

And now the entertainment began.

Into the arena formed by the tables floated a beautiful belly-dancer, an olive-skinned creature with a forty-four inch bust and hips to match. Hearty applause greeted her arrival and, encouraged by the mob's enthusiasm, she proceeded to give her all. By gum, she didn't half go at it, everything shaking and wobbling like half a ton of table jelly in a coal sifter.

A couple of minutes of this and her hands went behind her back. Snick! Off came her bra. The camera zoomed in and the screen was filled with stupendous knockers, her nipples sticking out hard as dum-dum bullets.

Now a shot of the crowd, showing the men's lascivious approval and one or two hands plunging down one or two necklines.

The party was hotting up – and so was I. I felt Gerta's

side-long glance at me but I didn't respond, just grinned at the screen and kept watching, my heart-beat rocking the bed.

Back to the belly-dancer. Moving round the tables as she danced, she began to abandon her veils one by one, throwing them at the male members of the audience who were clamouring for them, urging her on. Soon she was down to a mere three or four and through the sheer material her naked body was visible.

Another one floated across the tables . . . and another . . . a third . . . now she turned towards camera, her pubes scantily veiled by a single drape. Tauntingly she danced closer . . . closer . . . and then, in big close-up, she whipped away the final curtain and filled the screen with thick, black short-and-curlies.

Gerta exploded a laugh.

My heart was thundering. I took a swig of champers and the glass rattled against my teeth.

On the screen the blokes in the audience were beginning to get down to business. Several of the birds were now topless and one or two had their skirts up around their waists. Generally speaking, though, the night was still young.

Now into the arena came an acrobatic act, two luscious white-skinned lovelies in scanty Arabian outfits, and a huge, magnificently-built negro in a skimpy toga, thighs bristling with corded muscle and biceps like jelly moulds.

For a frame or two the team embarked on a conventional acrobatic routine, the birds standing on his thighs, on his shoulders, now all three forming a totem pole, but soon they abandoned this pretence and got down to it. As the negro held one girl aloft, the other fell to her knees and began stroking his thigh, now pecking it with kisses, slowly working her way higher and higher as though tormenting him during the execution of his serious acrobatic act.

'Stop it!' he protested, grinning down at her.

'Get lost,' she replied, continuing her ministrations.

Up and up she went, kissing, pecking, tickling . . . and suddenly his toga began to rise.

A close-up of the sweating negro, gritting his teeth.

Close-ups of the crowd, watching with bated breath.

Back to the toga. It was now standing out at right-angles and still rising. Gleefully Kneeling Nellie slid her hand up inside it and began to stroke. Up and up went the sporran of cloth, rising to a height I knew was ludicrously impossible. She was doing it . . . with her hand. Wasn't she!

Suddenly, she took hold of the flap and ripped it aside, tore it right away, revealing the most stupendous erection, a great throbbing rolling-pin of a cock that brought the crowd to its feet with thunderous applause.

Close-ups of girls, wide-eyed with wonder.

Close-ups of men, teeth gritted with envy.

Meanwhile, back to Kneeling Nellie, now joined by her pal from up aloft, the two of them playing on his cock like a flute, one each side, though the damn thing was long enough to have accommodated both on the same side with enough left over for an oboe solo.

'I don't believe it,' I gasped. 'It can't be real.'

Gerta roared with laughter, spilling her drink. 'Oh, it can. I have seen one that long . . . in a Hamburg nightclub.'

'Good God, have you really? What did he do with it?'

'Four negresses . . . one after the other.'

I gaped at her.

'You should see your face,' she laughed.

'I'd like to have seen the faces of those negresses!'

She laughed again and put out her hand to pat mine consolingly, 'Don't feel badly about it, size doesn't mean a thing . . . well, within reason.'

She turned her attention to the screen but did not remove her hand from mine. Instead, her fingers crept into my palm and she gave my hand a squeeze, then left it there.

Meanwhile, back at the orgy, things were getting rough. In a flurry of shots we saw wine being poured over breasts and licked off, men sprawled on top of women, buttocks rising and falling, a shot of a girl with a mouthful of boy-friend, another of a bird on top of a man . . . and as each shot appeared I got a communicative, almost reflex, squeeze from Gerta's hand.

I slid a glance at her. She was lost in concentration, eyes wide, lips parted, her breast rising and falling excitedly. She shifted her position, eased down into the cushions, raised one knee, causing the gown to fall wide open and now fully expose her legs. Did she realize it had happened? Had she done it purposely? Was she waiting for me to make a move?

My blood pounded. Herc was stuck down my trouser leg, hard as a board, incensed with the competition he'd seen on the screen and dying to give a good account of himself.

Gerta's mouth compressed in a smile and I flicked my eyes back to the screen in time to catch a noble Roman shed his nightie and fall upon a panting, supine maiden, driving his eight-inch sword into her in spectacular close-up.

From here on it was no-holds-barred. The starting flag had dropped for a knock-down, drag-out orgy and the extras were leaping to it with gusto. Clothing flew around the place like washing in a hurricane and before you could say 'sic transit clobber', the whole bleeding bunch were starkers.

By heck, the camera bloke really went to town now, fetching up shots of extremely penetrating observation – pun intended. He must have been more of a contortionist than his gymnastic subjects, to get the angles he got.

It was during a particularly artistic pillage of a ravishing red-head by a bloke with a gigantic cucumber that Gerta finally lost control. With sinister stealth our hero advanced on the terrified maiden, whose eyes were standing out on stalks, mortified by the size of his cock, yet who inexplicably was lying with her thighs as wide open as barn doors, begging for it. He dropped to his knees between her legs, lined up his torpedo on her cherry and with tortuous slowness fed it in . . . in . . . into her until he hit the buffers with a clang.

'My God . . .' I heard Gerta gasp, her nails biting into

the palm of my hand. I turned to look at her, found her looking at me, her eyes wild, excited, imploring.

Then she came at me, hit me with breathless kisses as her hand snaked down to locate Herc. 'Oh, sweet man, you're so hard, so big! Quickly!'

Feverishly she attacked my shirt, my trousers, hauling them off and flinging them across the room. For a brief suspended moment she became still, stared down at my bulging shorts, then, with a breathy cry of delight, hooked her fingers into the waistband and slowly drew the offending garment down.

Boing!

My old mate twanged northwards and slapped me on the belly.

'Wonderful!' she gasped, hurling the shorts over her shoulder. Quickly she rose up on her knees, slipped the buttons of her gown, flung it from her shoulders and tossed it into limbo. My brain exploded. She was sensationally naked. What a body . . . a big, strong, soft, voluptuous, fleshy . . .

She fell upon me, crushed me with her big, hot breasts, rolled on me, thrust Herc between her legs and squirmed all over me. Now she shot down the bed and slid Herc into her mouth, sucked and kissed and licked him all over, then quickly rose up, straddled me, guided him into the hot wet darkness between her legs, sucking in air as he drove high up into her and she finally came to rest across my thighs.

'Oh, *God* that is wonderful!' she cried, her eyes closed, teeth clenched. She caught my hands and pressed them to her breasts, thrusting her nipples between my thumbs and forefingers. 'Squeeze, darling, squeeze . . . hurt me, hurt me! Oh, my God, I'm coming . . . I'M COMING! . . .'

She let go a bellow, one rip-roaring thunder-clap of sound, and began a furious rocking against my bursting mate. Her lips twisted in a grimace of on-coming ecstasy, and then she was shouting again as another orgasm overwhelmed her. 'Ohhhh! Ohhhhh! *OHHHHHHH*!!'

She shook, shuddered, jerked into me, drove her clitoris

into my iron-hard root . . . then with a last massive, spasmic twitch, slumped.

For a moment she remained still, her face hidden by a curtain of hair, then suddenly she looked up, her eyes shining, laughing, ready to continue the game. She rose up from me, leaned over me to turn off the projector, then slid down beside me, her hand coming to rest on old Fatso.

'You didn't come, did you?' she murmured, nibbling my ear, tickling it with her tongue.

'No.'

'Why?'

'I knew you'd want more.'

She chuckled throatily. 'You're fantastic, you know that? Of course you do, you've been told a thousand times. Hey . . .'

'What?' I grinned.

She rolled on to her back, legs spread wide, arms extended towards me. 'Come here, I want you.'

I moved on top of her, slid Herc into her, so quickly it made her smile. 'He knows his way home.' She gave him a squeeze, frowning at the sensation. 'Oh, how beautiful that is . . .' She heaved a contented sigh and surged against me, coming to the boil again. 'I'm going to come again . . . no, don't move, let me do it . . . you just hang on there . . .' A stifled cry broke from her lips. She rolled her head, drove her fingers into my buttocks, hauling me hard up into her as she ground down on Herc and suddenly it was upon her. 'Oh, baby, baby . . . oh, my God . . . ohhhhh . . . OHHHHHHH! JESUS . . . I've come, I've come . . .'

Expelling a great billow of breath she collapsed beneath me, her arms flopping to the bed as she groaned comically, 'Oh, you naughty boy, what are you doing to me? Whatever it is, I love it, I love it, I love it.'

She opened her eyes and smiled at me, stroked my hair, prodded me on the nose. 'Oh, I wish I'd sent for that projector months ago, I've needed this for an awfully long time. I see that surprises you.'

'I'm surprised you have no lovers. You're a *very* attractive woman.'

'Thank you . . . but I have to be careful. My husband . . . I think he's having me watched. I'm divorcing him for adultery and he would love to be able to counter-claim against me for the same thing.'

'I see.'

Her eyes changed, became hot again, and once more she moved against me. 'You have the most fantastic control,' she purred sexily. 'You must have had a great deal of experience.'

I grinned. 'You don't know how hard I'm having to fight.'

She touched my face. 'Poor lamb, I'm being terribly selfish, aren't I? All right, then, you shall have your reward . . .'

Her legs came up and encircled me. She thrust into me, drew away, got the rhythm going. 'Oh, that is gorgeous . . . drive him home . . . hard, baby, hard . . .' Her breathing erupted in a gasp and her fingers became claws in my back. 'Go, baby, go . . . fuck me . . . fill me! FILL ME! Ohhhh . . . Ohhhhh . . . OHHHHHH!'

BarrrrroooOOOOOMMMMM! The heavens opened. Her eyes flew wide, she clutched my face and kissed me. 'Beautiful . . . beautiful . . . Oh, how sweet that is! I love it, I love it!'

She collapsed laughing, and I collapsed on top of her, gasping for breath.

'There, there . . .' she chuckled, stroking my back, my neck, my hair. 'Now we have really made love. Relax . . . lie still . . . get your strength back and we will go into the lounge, play some nice music and have a drink. Would you like that?'

'Yes,' I panted, 'I'd like that.'

Gradually we calmed, became quite still.

'I knew it would be like this,' she said softly, 'I made up my mind to seduce you the moment I opened the door. This is a very sexy man, I said to myself, and I would like very much to go to bed with him.'

'I'm very glad,' I grinned, kissing her breast.

'Ah, I see you have recovered.'

'Getting there.'

'Come . . . we shall have a shower together, I will find you a robe to wear, and we shall have a nice quiet drink. I shall also make us something to eat, you must be hungry after all your hard work.'

'Getting there, too.'

'Good,' she smiled. 'We must restore you to full health and strength before you go home.'

CHAPTER TWELVE

My suspicions that I'd encountered a woman of gargantuan sexual appetite, landed a right raver, began not many minutes after we'd vacated the bed and taken up residence in the bathroom – no mere bathroom, more of a flat within a flat, a mirrored stateroom of regal proportions and palatial gilt-and-marble furnishings, incorporating a pool-size sunken bath, a sauna, a shower cubicle large enough to accommodate a rugger team, ultra-violet sun-lamp beds, and several lounging sofas, the whole schmeer carpeted in rich, white, ankle-deep pile and demanding to be used in imaginative dalliance.

'Wey hey . . .' I remarked as we entered, Gerta triggering a wall switch which bathed the naughty room in soft, pink lighting, a further encouragement to dally with lascivious licence in the nod.

Holding my hand she led me into the centre of the room, her smile indicating her amusement with the images of our naked selves, reflected, at a dozen different angles, in the huge pink mirrors lining the walls and ceiling.

'A handsome couple?' she suggested pertly, inflating her breasts and preeningly posing before one of the mirrors.

I looked at our image, experiencing a stirring of the loins at this unique, vicarious observation of our joint nakedness, the juxtaposition of our sex organs stimulating a vivid realization of what they were for and a piercing desire to put them precisely to that use.

Gerta was obviously and simultaneously afflicted by the same urge, for she unveiled a smile at me, telling me she knew what I was thinking, and slowly turned to embrace me, grinning at me as Herc rose stiffly, in the flush of renewed and intense excitement, against her belly.

She kissed me, moaned appreciatively and pressed

against him, now slowly fell to her knees and enveloped him with her velvet lips, driving me cuckoo with her playful, flicking tongue.

'You like that, baby?' she murmured, kissing, pecking, tickling.

All around me a multitude of Gerta's were doing the same thing. It was an unbelievable moment.

She stood up and plastered a wet kiss on my mouth, smiling at me through veiled, lecherous eyes, then, laughing, took my hand and led me to the huge bath.

Releasing a plunger, she turned on two enormous gilt taps, shaped like swans, and water cascaded into the pool under tremendous pressure. While it filled, she returned her attention to me, embraced me, rubbed her nose against mine and murmured, 'I'm so glad you came.'

I ran my hands down her flesh, relishing its velvet softness, and took hold of her buttocks. 'So am I,' I grinned, my voice quavery, my body trembling.

'I want to play with you all night.'

'Do you? What do you want to play?'

She shrugged. 'Just play . . . do whatever comes to mind. There's no one else in the world tonight, just us two. There's no one watching . . . no one listening . . . we can do whatever we like.'

'Yes,' I grinned.

'Come . . . you shall wash me and I shall wash you. And if we feel like it we shall stay in here all night.'

She turned away, shut off the taps, dipped her toe in the water, then slid into it, up to her waist, and beckoned me in.

From a tray dispenser set in the side of the bath she poured green and blue unctions into the water and whipped them into clouds of perfumed bubbles, then from the tray took a bar of soap and a big sea sponge and held them out to me.

'You first.'

I worked up a rich lather and began on her back, drawing a sensuous moan from her as I trickled spongefuls of lubricated water down her spine.

'That's gorgeous . . . you must stay here for ever and do this to me every day.'

'All right. I shall be your butler, handyman, bath attendant . . . and whatever else you conjure up.'

She laughed. 'I could think of lots of things. I would enjoy waking and finding you in my bedroom, my breakfast on a tray . . .' She turned to face me, her hand sneaking underwater to capture Herc, '. . . except the breakfast would go cold because I'd pull you into bed and make a meal of *him*.'

'Hey . . .'

'How big he grows.' She looked down, smiling, watching him pop up out of the water like a periscope. Then she mounted me, slid Herc right up inside her and embraced me, curling her legs around my waist. 'Oh, that is beautiful . . .'

'I'm supposed to be washing you,' I said, dropping the soap and sponge to hold her.

She kissed my neck, nibbled my ear, bit the lobe. 'I feel awfully *sexy*, I can't get enough of you. Make me come, darling . . .'

It wasn't difficult. Three or four deep strokes and she was away, gasping in my ear, her fingers tearing into my hair. '*Ohhh*, my God . . . ohhh! OHHHH! . . .'

She clung tightly to me, her body coiled like a spring, then, with a grunt, relaxed on me. 'Wow . . .'

'That sounded a good one,' I chuckled.

'That was a *gorgeous* one. You do it so beautifully.'

She unwound herself and immersed herself in the water, sat on the bottom of the bath and leaned back against the side, her head thrown back and eyes closed, a smile on her lips. 'This is heaven . . . heaven . . . heaven.'

I lay beside her, almost floating. 'It's certainly a long way from Balham.'

'You can't go on living there, Russ, you deserve better than that.'

I shrugged. 'Everything takes money. Oh, I have very definite ideas about the life-style I'd choose . . . this comes pretty close to it. But how do you achieve it without money?'

'You must earn more.'

I nodded. 'I know, but it's not easy when you start from scratch. They say your first million is the hardest, but it's more simple than that – your first ten thousand is the hardest.'

'It will take you a long time to earn that selling projectors,' she smiled.

'Oh, this is just a stop-gap, Gerta, a desperation measure. I did earn quite a lot of money doing television commercials a couple of years ago, but spent it travelling round the world. When I got back from Ireland I discovered, to my horror, I'd miscalculated. I thought I had a few hundred left, but it had all gone and I was two pounds overdrawn.'

She laughed. 'You sound as clever as I am with money.' She looked at me, studied my face. 'You're a handsome man, you should do well for yourself. You are nice to be with. I know fifty women who would adore to be in my position right now.' She looked away, inspected her toes. 'The world is full of bored, lonely, wealthy women, Russ.'

'Who look like you? Have your sense of fun?' I shook my head. 'There w uldn't be another one like you, Gerta, and I couldn't do this with just anyone. I'd make a lousy gigolo. I couldn't do this for money.'

'Thank you for that,' she said softly, reaching to squeeze my hand. She stood up, a sculpture of twinkling soap suds. 'I think we're clean enough, let's go and get a drink.'

In the lounge, she in her oyster gown, me in a robe of midnight blue silk, she mixed two vodka tonics and came to sit beside me on cushions she'd thrown on the floor in front of the fire. With our backs to the settee, we drank our drinks and stared into the crackling fire, divorced from reality, enjoying each other.

'Tell me about the television commercials,' she said. 'Would I have seen them?'

'Possibly. I was presenting for White Marvel detergent, doing street interviews with housewives. I hear they're still going out, but I shouldn't think too often now. The main campaign would have gone out last year.'

She shook her head, frowning thoughtfully. 'No, I don't think I've seen them. I was living abroad most of last year.' She smiled. 'Were you good? I'm sure you were.'

'The client liked them.'

'Why don't you do more commercials now?'

'I couldn't – not while the White Marvels are still going out. It's one of the penalties of the business, I'm afraid, you can succeed yourself out of it.'

'Yes, I can see that. Have you ever thought of acting, Russ?'

'I've been tempted, but times are against it . . . at least in this country.'

'How about abroad? America, for instance?'

'The odds would be pretty long for an English accent.'

'But there's a lot more work out there. And I've heard quite a few English accents in American TV series lately, they seem to be using them to attract British viewers.' She glanced at me, then down at her glass, playfully running her finger round the rim, smiling provocatively. 'I know some people in Hollywood.'

I shot a look at her. 'You do?'

'Hm hm . . . I could put you in touch with them if you fancied a trip out there. Nothing may come of it, of course, but it might be worth a try.'

I laughed, taken aback by this unexpected turn of events. 'Yes, it might. But wouldn't I need a work permit . . . an immigration visa?'

She shrugged. 'They can be got. I have many friends in many places, there have to be *some* advantages to being married to a duke, a count and a baron. But in any case, you could go out initially on a holiday visa.'

'Yes,' I said, thinking about it, intrigued by the prospect. Oh, not so much by any fanciful expectation of becoming an overnight Superstar, but by the mere thought of a trip to Hollywood.

Truth to tell, I'd been suffering pangs of wanderlust lately, been feeling the stirrings to be up and away again.

I'd been back in this hemisphere for six months now and the novelty was beginning to pall. Yes, Hollywood would fill the bill nicely. Actually, it was a place that had always intrigued me, somewhere I'd always wanted to see, and it had been something of a disappointment not to have visited it when I'd been in Las Vegas with Buzz Malone. We'd been very close to Los Angeles then, only an hour's flying time, but we hadn't been able to make it.

'What are you thinking?' she asked.

'I'm thinking you might have hit on something. I'm a believer in exposing oneself to life, pardon the expression...'

She laughed.

'It's been my experience,' I went on, 'that things begin to happen when you step out into the world – at least they do to me. And Hollywood sounds the sort of place where things happen to people more than most other places.'

'True,' she smiled, 'I can certainly vouch for that. I spent one of the most amazing years of my life out there. Granted, it did help being the wife of an Italian count, but for almost anybody it's still perhaps the most "happening" town in the world. I think *you'd* have a whale of a time there . . . particularly with one or two addresses I could give you.'

My pulse quickened. 'Oh? What sort of addresses?'

A saucy smile. 'Oh . . . girlfriends of mine. They'd adore you.'

'Really. And what do these girlfriends *do* in Hollywood?'

She leaned towards me and pecked me on the mouth. 'Gorgeous men like you, mostly. You'd have a wonderful time.'

She got to her feet to replenish our drinks and put on another LP, saying over her shoulder. 'I can see the idea appeals to you.'

'Oh, it appeals to me. I'm just wondering how long it would take me to save up the money. I reckon I'd need at least five hundred pounds and that would take me a good three months to save.'

'September. Well, that's as good a month as any to be in California.'

I laughed. 'You know, it's so refreshing talking to you, Gerta, you make world conquest sound so simple.'

She returned with the drinks, knelt at my side and gave me mine. Looking at her, her blonde hair loose and free, a mischievous twinkle in her eye, it suddenly occurred to me she looked years younger than when I'd arrived. She was really having fun.

I'd met women like her before, women who had married money, position, title, and had inherited loneliness, boredom and loss of youthful fun. It was understandable that they needed to break out, to enjoy mad, irresponsible, do-as-you-damn-well-please evenings like this now and again. I was just delighted I was the one to knock on her door.

'World conquest *can* be simple,' she answered. 'Provided you're equipped for the job. And you are.'

'You really think so, hm?'

'I *know* so,' she laughed. 'Who should know better! I know many men who have done very well for themselves with far less going for them than you have. All you need is to meet the right people – at the right time and in the right place.'

'A problem, as with acquiring money, when you start from scratch.'

'Nevertheless, it's not too late to start now.'

I frowned at her, smilingly. 'You really sound convinced that big things could be waiting for me out there somewhere. I must say it's all very exciting.'

She came back to her original position, sitting beside me, closer now. 'What do you really want from life, Russ?'

I thought about it. 'Funny thing, Gerta, but when you start life as I started it – in a working-class terraced house, just enough schooling to get by, an office job in the Liverpool docks – you don't think in terms of specifics. You're just propelled along, day by day, by a general ambition to get the hell out, to improve yourself, travel, acquire position, money, fame, comforts. And you get so used to living with these generalities. you're really quite stumped when somebody asks you what you *specifically* want out of life.'

I shrugged. 'I guess it mostly hinges on money, doesn't it? With enough of that in the bank you've got time, and freedom, to think, plan, decide, try different things out. I remember the dilemma I was faced with when I worked in that office in the Liverpool docks, hating every minute of it and needing to get out to save *my* sanity. I couldn't afford to quit, to be out of work – so how could I find another job? I was lucky a selling job came along through a pal of mine at the cricket club, otherwise I might still have been stuck in Wainwright's – or dead by now of galloping boredom.'

She laughed, put a sympathetic hand on my knee. 'I know. But don't you have a vision of the life-style you'd like to enjoy?'

'Yes, when I put my mind to it. I'm a sun-worshipper, I love to see it shining, brightening up the world. I don't need it to be too hot, nor to be actually in it, but I like it around me, so I can spend the day in shirtsleeves and shorts. I loved Africa for that reason.'

I smiled, 'Now that you've asked me, I sometimes see myself as owning a boatyard in the Bahamas, renting out cabin cruisers, repairing them, perhaps even building them. I see myself pottering around in the sunshine, taking out a fishing party into the Caribbean, warm trade-winds and a cloudless blue sky. That's how I see myself.' I laughed. 'Not much to ask for, is it?'

'No, it isn't,' she said seriously. 'So why haven't you gone after that sort of life?'

'Ohh . . . I did actually get to the Bahamas, had a lot of fun there, too, but somehow I just kept going. Somehow the next place along the road always seems to hold out greater promise of interest, adventure, excitement.'

'You're an incorrigible romantic . . .' she smiled, caressing my knee. 'Also you haven't seen enough of the world to want to settle down yet. Don't let it worry you, you're young enough, you've got plenty of time.'

'Oh, it doesn't worry me – only this everlasting shortage

of money worries me. If I had a cool hundred thousand I wouldn't have a worry in the world!'

We lapsed into thoughtful silence for a moment, then, with a nod, she said, 'I really think you ought to try Hollywood, Russ. The very least you'd get out of it is sunshine, but I've got a feeling you'd come out with a lot more than that . . .' She smiled, '. . . even if it was only a wealth of experience.'

'I'm sure you're right, Gerta. You've done it now, you know, I won't be able to think of anything but Hollywood from now on. I won't have any heart for selling Zip appliances.' I sighed. 'I'll have to, though, if I'm going to raise the money.'

She leaned into me and kissed my cheek, nibbled my ear. 'Perhaps I can help you . . . for being such a good boy.'

Up went the pulse rate. She was getting horny again.

'Oh?' I croaked.

'Kiss me.'

Her mouth was soft, urgently pliant. My heart began a tattoo and Herc stirred mightily from slumber. Her hand crept inside my robe and felt my body, then dropped to the loosely-tied sash, unfastened it, at the same time she leaned against me, easing me down into the cushions.

She rained playful kisses on my chest, neck, stomach . . . her hand simutaneously creeping up my leg to capture Herc in a tender grasp.

'He's so big . . . so beautiful,' she murmured, running her lips down my stomach. And into her molten mouth he popped.

Without losing him, she shrugged her gown from her shoulders and, as it dropped behind her, I removed it and threw it on the settee. How beautiful she was in the rosy firelight, her breasts, her skin – glowing, perfect, satin smooth.

Now she came to lie beside me, her eyes heavy-lidded, her arms outstretched, beseeching, and wordlessly I rolled between her legs and entered her.

'Oh, Russ, that's beautiful,' she gasped, stroking my face, my hair. 'He feels so hard, so strong up there . . . I feel so *full* of you.' Savagely, she grabbed a handful of hair and growled between gritted teeth, 'Fuck me, you devil . . . hard! Rape me! . . . RAPE ME! . . .'

She went berserk, threw her loins up into me into a wild frenzy, taking each thrust with a stifled cry, driving me violently into her, bellowing sweet obscenities at me, urging me on, exciting me beyond belief, bringing me almost immediately to monumental orgasm as she herself exploded with one gargantuan climax and a shout of jubilation that they must have heard in Brighton.

Now she broke into laughter . . . helpless, joyous, chuckling laughter, flinging her arms out wide, then rushing them back to squeeze the breath from my body. 'Oh, you . . . LOVER! That was fantastic . . . incredible!' she gasped, breasts heaving against my chest. 'I adore you . . . thank you . . . thank you . . . I just needed you . . . *hard* . . . *brutally*! It was perfect.'

I lay for a long while in her arms, on the soft, heavenly mattress of her body, reflecting with wonderment how good love-making can be when the moment and the chemistry are right, knowing she was thinking the same thing.

'I wish I'd met you when I was nineteen,' she murmured softly, lazily stroking my back. Then she laughed. 'No, perhaps you'd have been a *bit* too young then . . . though I don't doubt you were beginning to show remarkable promise at the age of nine!'

'Seven, actually,' I joked.

'I don't doubt it. I should think you were born with an erection . . . *and* knew how to use it.'

'It does save valuable time. Terrible waste – not doing anything with it until you're in your twenties.'

She squirmed into me, undulating her pelvis. 'You're certainly making up for it. I've had my year's quota in one night.'

'Not really.'

She grinned. 'Perhaps not quite . . . though it's been a very lean time lately with my husband's spies on the loose.'

‘Are you serious? Do you really think he’s having you watched?’

‘Yes, I’m being very careful until the divorce comes through.’ She smiled. ‘That’s why you were a particular godsend tonight . . . though I didn’t expect it to be this good.’ She looked at me, tenderly. ‘I’ll have to think of something very special for you.’

‘I don’t want anything, Gerta . . .’

‘Ssshh . . .’ she placed a finger on my lips. ‘Don’t be so male chauvinist independent, take help where you can get it. I’m not talking about money, I’m talking about . . . well, never you mind. Give me your address when you go . . . if you ever *plan* on going, that is. Or do you have it in mind to stay in me for ever? You know something?’

‘What’s that?’

‘I promised to feed you about twelve hours ago. Now you *must* be starved.’

CHAPTER THIRTEEN

The coach, drawn by four black horses, rattled to a halt at the main door of the castle and the girl alighted. Barely had her poor luggage been handed down by the driver when he whipped the horses into movement, anxious to be gone from this grim and haunted place.

The girl, clothed from head to feet in a bonnet, cape and long skirts, peered apprehensively up at the towering granite battlements, then at a piece of paper in her hand, then picked up her valise and made her way up stone steps to the massive iron-studded door.

Tugging on a bell-pull, she waits, the camera revealing, in close-up, that she is indeed a young and extremely comely wench.

Slow, creakingly, the huge door opens. The craggy, decrepit face of an aged retainer appears. He looks her up and down, takes the proffered piece of paper, studies it, then, with a nod, beckons her in.

CUT TO: The hall – lofty, cheerless place of granite walls and floor. The girl enters, peering about her with the gravest apprehension. The retainer, a tall, sepulchral creature in kilt and sporran, points aloft. The camera, representing her point of view, pans around the hall and up an endless staircase of granite steps, spiralling upwards to a tower.

Close-up of retainer, mouthing at her, followed by a title card which says 'Go tae your room, lass. Your duties as scullery maid start at 5 a.m. tomorrae mornin'.'

'Poor thing,' laughed Gerta. 'Do people *really* get up at 5 a.m.?'

'You're asking the wrong fella,' I grinned. 'I didn't know there was such a time. You look disturbingly ravishing lying there.'

'Ssshh . . . watch the film.'

In long-shot we see the poor wretch dejectedly climb the stairs. Then, as she nears the top, the camera pans slowly round . . . and stops . . . as a new face fills the screen, a malevolent face, the face of a debaucher, a despoiler of women, a cruel yet handsome swine.

With flaring, lecherous eyes he watches the progress of the girl, then, with a twisted smirk and a fingering of his moustache, he walks out of frame, a mid-shot showing him, also kilted, beginning to climb the stairs.

CUT TO: The wench's room, a dismal tower room, boasting little comfort other than a four-poster bed and a wash-hand-stand.

'Looks familiar,' I commented. 'Reminds me of home.'

'In Balham? You're joking.'

I grinned at her. 'No.'

The girl crosses to the window and looks down, her shoulders slumping. So all alone, so far from home. Wearily she crosses to the bed, sits on it, and begins to undress.

Off comes her bonnet. She shakes out her hair, a magnificent cascade of copper-coloured tresses. Now her cape, revealing a pair of breasts the size of honeydew melons bursting out of her bodice. Snick . . . snick . . . the bodice is unlaced. She stands up, drops one skirt . . . then another . . . yet another . . . and while all this is going on – or coming off – the camera pans away to reveal her door furtively opening.

Yes, it's none other than Dirty Dick, the unprincipled swine, grabbing a butcher's on the QT. In huge close-up his eyes flare monstrously and his tongue flicks across his parched and prurient lips.

Reverse shot – his viewpoint. No wonder he's getting all hot and bothered because at that very moment Dishpan Doris has removed her vest and is parading her stupendous honeydews, pips and all. By gum, they are a sight for sore eyes – and Dirty Richard obviously agrees.

Boing! go his peepers, wobbling in their sockets.

Greta laughed and snuggled into me, really enjoying herself.

But soft . . . our villain's breath is now coming in short pants.

Doris, obviously feeling the heat, is stepping out of her bloomers, leaving only an anachronistic black suspender belt and black silk stockings which excitingly frame her thick red swatch of pubic undergrowth.

This is more than Filthy Richard can stand. With one bound he is in the room, frightening the life out of the poor kid with an erection that has transformed his Black Watch kilt into a Chipperfield big top tent.

'Aaaaagghh . . .' she cries, backing towards the bed, trying futilely to cover her umpteen private parts with an insufficient number of arms. 'Get out of here, you . . . you . . .'

More abominable eye-flaring and moustache-twiddling from Dick.

'What do you want of me, a poor defenceless scullery maid?' pleads Doris.

'Are you kidding?' scoffs Dick, his hands flying to his sporran.

Down zooms his kilt to his feet. So – it's true what they say about Scotsmen! All Dick is wearing under the tartan is a cock the length of his claymore and a pair of cannonballs hefty enough to blow holes in the walls of Edinburgh Castle.

Doris stares, transfixed, as Raunchy Richard advances on her, acutely resembling a unicorn at full gallop.

'On the bed wi' ye, lass!' he demands.

'Never, never! Take the beastly thing away!'

'Ye cannae refuse – it's the master's perks wi' the new hired help!'

'I shall chuck myself out of the window rather than submit to *that*!'

Gerta sighed impatiently. 'What's the matter with her? Doesn't she *know* what's good for her.'

Her hand trickled playfully up my thigh. 'She doesn't know what she's missing,' she chuckled.

'I've got a feeling she's soon going to find out. Stop that and watch the film.'

She continued doing both.

As D.D. clutches the wench by the shoulders and sinks his teeth into her neck, the camera *CUTS TO*: The entrance hall downstairs.

Through the front door bursts our kilted hero, Peter Pure, with clean knees and a halo of golden curls. Grabbing the senile retainer by the lapels, he shakes the daylights – and the information – out of him. The retainer points a shaking finger up the stairs.

'The master's havin' his wicked way with her this very instant!'

Hurling the old fool aside, Pete races up the stairs three at a time, bent on rescue.

Meanwhile, back in the tower, Dastardly Dick, having failed to impress Doris with his charm, wit, personality and sense of boyish fun, has resorted to the only other reasonable alternative – brute force. And Doris is now pegged out on the bed like a beached starfish, her ankles and wrists secured to the four corner posts by cruel iron manacles.

'What-ho, me beauty,' leers Dick, ogling her rusty rift with randy rapacity. 'Prepare to meet *this*!'

He scrambles up on the bed and kneels between her wide-spread legs, his trusty claymore in both hands.

Reverse shot – Doris' eyeline. Good God, no wonder the kid's worried. From this angle he looks like a champion caber-tosser about to let fly.

'Oh, dear . . .' murmured Gerta. 'She's got troubles.'

'So will you if you don't stop doing that.'

'Promises, promises.'

Doris struggles . . . my, how she struggles . . . bucks and tosses and flings her hips in the air, which, from Richard's point-of-view, is precisely what she shouldn't be doing!

What red-blooded Highland sport can possibly resist the challenge of a moving target?

'Tally-ho!' he cries, lining up his ludicrous lance on her leaping lily . . . and down he plunges.

But no!

Before he can drive his devastating dildo into her dodging daisy, the door flies open and into the room bounds good old Pete.

'STOP! Plunge not your puissant pole into that poor peasant's propinquitous pussy or you'll answer to Peter Pure!'

'Get knotted,' retorts Richard, still trying to get it in.

'Then be it on your own head!' cries Pete, seizing a brass bed-warmer from the wall.

Boing!

He lets Dick have it flush on the noggin.

Dick rolls off the bed and collapses on the floor, lucky not to have run himself through with his own claymore.

'My hero!' cries Doris.

'Beloved!' replies Pete, releasing her in a trice from her cruel manacles.

She embraces him. Her hand flies up his kilt as a gesture of appreciation. In feverish haste, Pete is up on his knees, hurling away his kilt.

She gapes . . . in horror . . . mortified by his puny pudenda, scarcely bigger than her little finger.

In one bound she's off the bed. He is after her, begging, pleading, apologizing. Furious, she rounds on him with the bed-warmer.

Boing!

Cross-eyed, he sinks to the floor, out for the night.

She is appalled at what she's done. In desperation she searches the room, her eye alighting on a water pitcher on the washhand-stand. She streaks for it, stands over recumbent Pete . . . then, with a cruel laugh, turns to Dick and lets him have it in the mush.

He comes-to. She helps him up, then leaps on the bed and refastens the cruel iron manacles around her own ankles.

'Ravage me!' she begs.

And with an insidious leer at camera, Dick obliges.

'There's a moral there somewhere,' said Gerta, rising above me on her knees to switch off the projector. 'But I can't quite put my finger on it.'

'No comment. Do you know, you look delectably edible from down here.'

'You've already eaten.'

'Only the main course, I didn't have dessert.'

'Sweets for the sweet,' she grinned, descending.

It was after midnight when she saw me to the door. 'Well, thank you, madam,' I joked. 'Be assured I shall meet all after-sales service requirements with an alacrity *way* beyond the normal call of duty.'

'Thank you, Mr Tobin. And something tells me this projector is going to break down with tiresome frequency.'

I shrugged. 'It happens. Every now and then we do get a bad one. Still, it can't be helped.'

She kissed me. 'Thank you. Dare I say you've saved my sanity?'

'You – can say what you like.'

'I'll be in touch, I have your address.'

'And I have yours.'

She let me out, blew me a kiss, and closed the door.

Smiling to myself, I called up the elevator and rode down to reality. What an evening. It was hard to believe it had happened, and it grew increasingly hard to believe as I drove home along the wet, deserted midnight streets.

I entered the sleeping house, crept up the stairs, and lay down on my bed, disbelieving I'd been enjoying such opulence such a short time ago. With a sigh, I looked around the room, at the peeling wallpaper and cracked ceiling . . . oh boy, oh boy, how the mighty are fallen.

All that had happened seemed ridiculous now, all that talk of Hollywood, the people she knew. Nothing would come of it, I knew.

I got off the bed and undressed, went down to the bathroom (this was a bathroom!) then returned and put out the light.

Hollywood?

Well, certainly not tomorrow. Tomorrow it was back to food mixers and kettles and Mrs Barrys of Paradise Roads and . . .

I grinned to myself. Well, to hell with all that *until* tomorrow. Tonight it was going to be nothing but sweet memories.

And with her perfume on my pillow, I fell asleep.

CHAPTER FOURTEEN

The next morning, Saturday, Dennis couldn't wait until I got downstairs to tell me the news. He was knocking on my door before the alarm went off.

'Russ?' His head was in the door. 'Are you asleep?'

'Was, old kid. What's the matter – your bed on fire?'

He grinned. 'How did you know! Can I come in a minute?'

'Could have sworn you were in.' I put on the light and blinked at the alarm clock. 'Ten to seven! What's up with you, have you got a dem. to do in Glasgow or something?'

'Listen!' he squatted on the bed, 'I've got to tell you . . . I've met her!'

'Who?'

He pointed downstairs, his finger making like a woodpecker hammering at a tree. 'The mystery bird!' He rolled his eyes. 'Oh, man, wait till I tell you . . .'

I yawned massively. 'I'm waiting, Dennis.'

He moved closer, in a terrible state. 'I got home about six last night – had a *terrific* day . . .'

'You, too,' I grinned.

'Hm . . ? You did, too?'

'Never mind – carry on before you burst. I'll tell you about mine after.'

'Well, as I say, I got home about six . . . fantastic day, *four* Super vacuums, *two* Super mixers and a sewing machine!'

'Bloody marvellous.'

'Well, I wanted to tell you about it, and I didn't see your van outside, so I came upstairs to leave a note for you, telling you to knock on my door.'

I frowned. 'I didn't find it.'

'I know – because I didn't leave it. I didn't get up to your room.'

'Oh?'

'No, I got as far as *her* room . . . and found her door ajar. Funny, I thought, she's usually gone by six o'clock, so I sort of sidled up and had a squint.'

'Dirty, that.'

'Yeh.' He shook his head. 'You'll never guess what I saw.'

'She was milking an elephant.'

'Man, she had a tape-recorder on, playing soul music, and she was dancing to it – you know, this go-go stuff those birds do on Top of the Pops . . . all wiggling arms and pelvic jerks, and . . .' he rolled his eyes again, '. . . Christ, Russ, it was all going. But not only that – she was damn-near naked! She was wearing a gold-lamé bikini thing with tassles on it . . . just a titchy pair of knicks and a nothing bra. I damn-near died. Boy, is she built . . . fantastic body . . . wonderful skin . . . the colour of creamy coffee . . .'

'Steady, Den, you'll be having one on my bed. So what happened?'

'Well, I stood there like I'd been hit by a truck, didn't I? Couldn't take my eyes off her. I watched her dance one whole number, then she suddenly moved across the room to get a towel to wipe her face . . . and when she turned round, she saw me!'

'Oh, blimey . . .'

'Yeh, that's what I thought. I thought she'd blow me up, slam the door in my face . . .'

'But she didn't.'

'Did she heck. She just grinned and said, "Hi," cool as you like. Then she started chatting! Said she'd seen me before, asked me my name, told me hers was,' he grinned, 'you'll never believe it.'

'Strange name for a bird.'

'Devina Delmar!'

'I don't believe it.'

'I just told you you wouldn't. I said to her, "you're enjoying yourself," and she said, "no, I'm working, I'm rehearsing a new routine." Then – and this you *won't* believe, Russ – she asked me if I wanted to go in and watch!'

'You lucky stiff.'

'You're damn right I was.'

'What was she rehearsing for?'

He shrugged. 'To get better at it.'

'No, you narna, I mean . . . for a show or what?'

'Yeh, kind of,' he chuckled. 'Russ . . . she's a go-go dancer in a Soho club!'

'Blimey, some guys get all the luck. Well, go on, lay the gory details on me.'

'Oh, boy . . . I tell you, it was . . . well, there was I, lying on her bed, and there she was, wriggling and writhing that fantastic body, not giving a stuff that she was almost naked, and . . . well, anyway, she finished her routine and I expected her to say she was going to work . . .'

'But she didn't.'

'But she didn't. She told me to stay put while she had a bath, and when she came back she was wearing a dress. And then she said she was going out for something to eat and asked me if I'd like to join her!'

'Fantastic. Did she have the night off?'

'Yeh!'

'Where did you go?'

He frowned. 'A pub somewhere, I don't remember. I couldn't believe it was happening to me.'

'I know the feeling.'

'I mean, Russ, she's beautiful! I couldn't believe I was taking her out.'

'You weren't – she was taking you out. Don't question it, just keep saying the "Hail Marys" or sacrificing the goats or whatever you do. Who can fathom the machinations of the beautiful female mind? Proceed, Don Juan.'

'She's beautiful, Russ . . .'

'You've already said that.'

'No, I don't just mean physically, I mean . . . crikey, we talked for hours! Told me all about herself – she comes from Granada in the West Indies – but she's lived here for five years. And she wanted to know all about me . . .' he laughed, '. . . we talked so long they chucked us out at closing time. We never did get anything to eat.'

'And?'

He shrugged. 'And then we came home.'

'And?'

'I . . . saw her to her door.'

'And?'

'And . . . she asked me if I'd like to see the routine as she'll do it at the club.'

'And?'

He gulped. 'Russ . . . she works . . . topless.'

'Oh, brother.'

He shook his head. 'It was unbelievable. I've never seen such . . . out of this *world*, man . . .'

I laughed at him. He looked like a miner who'd just stumbled on the mother-lode. 'Congratulations, old son, looks like you're home and dry.'

'Hardly the description of what followed.'

'You *dirty* devil.'

He held out his hands. 'Look at them, they're still shaking! Four o'clock this morning we were still . . . you know.'

'That's disgusting. You mean you were actually *doing* it while I was creeping past her door at one o'clock this morning?'

He nodded, dumbly, then, realizing what I'd said, looked up sharply. 'What were you doing out till one this morning?'

I gave a nonchalant shrug and polished my nails on my naked chest. 'Oh . . . this and that, here and there. No, I'll tell you the truth, Dennis, I was demming a film projector.'

'At one in the morning? Come off it.'

'So – don't believe me.'

His eyes narrowed. 'I believe you. Who was she?'

'Who said it was a she?'

'Ho, tooty frooty. Nah, come on, stop messing about.'

Languidly I reclined against the pillows, hands behind my head. 'I have been contemplating a change of profession, Dennis. It has been put to me that I ought to try the acting profession.'

'Try it for what?'

'Acting, you chump!'

'Was she drunk? No, I'm only kidding . . . are you serious?'

I laughed. 'No, not really. I thought I was at the time, but now, in the cold light of day . . .' I sighed dramatically. 'Nevertheless, it was a most remarkable encounter – as obviously yours was. Incredible coincidence that we should both have struck oil on the same evening. The difference is, though, that yours stands a very good chance of being an on-going gusher – if you'll pardon the analogy . . .'

'Sure.'

'Whereas mine . . .'

'Pumped dry?' he suggested.

'Don't be filthy. No, different drilling operation altogether, Dennis . . . complicated by husbands and things.'

'Oh. Still, sounds like you had one terrific evening, mate.'

'One *heck* of an evening . . .'

The alarm went off, making us jump. I smashed it in the head and Dennis got up. 'Don't know whether I can face the animals this morning. I think maybe I'll eat breakfast at the diner.'

'Mind if I join you?'

'Delighted.'

It was a rotten morning, weather-wise and business-wise. The rain continued to fall in a solid sheet, drenching me every time I got out of the van, getting down into my collar and soaking through my shoes, and the calls I had to make didn't improve matters, all of them in the East End, a million miles from the glamour of Roehampton, and all of them piddling bits and pieces – a kettle, a hair-dryer, a toaster and a steam iron.

Nothing seemed to go right. The first two customers were out shopping, not surprising since it was Saturday morning, the third was a no-no because she'd changed her mind about a Zip appliance since sending in the coupon and she'd already bought a Sunbeam toaster. And the fourth thought the Zip steam iron was too expensive.

Spiritlessly, I doubled back on the customers who'd been out shopping and managed to flog a Super kettle to the first one; but the second, the hair-dryer, turned out to be a drunken old bag with hair like chewed string, and I finished up recommending she needed a transplant, not a dryer, and she threw me out.

Well, that was it, I'd had enough for one week. I drove back to Zip to collect my earnings, the one bright spot on the day's horizon, but even that was a stupendous let-down.

Oh, sure, Polkoski congratulated me on a most successful first week and said he felt I had a great future with Zip and joked about me buying him out, the way I was going . . . but then he handed me my cheque and it all fell to pieces.

It was my own fault, of course, for not calculating what the deductions would be. I'd been floating along all week in a filthy capitalist euphoria, refusing to face the harsh reality of deductions, thinking only in terms of gross earnings, which, according to my estimation, were up around the one hundred and ten pounds mark. So when he handed me a cheque for only thirty-seven quid I deflated like a punctured inner-tube.

'Thirty-seven?' I frowned, smitten by shock, dismay, disappointment, grief.

It was there on the slip of paper. Income Tax deduction, Social Security deduction, Van Hire deduction, Petrol deduction . . . deduction, deduction, deduction . . . and all the rest was mine.

The only good thing about it all was that, being Saturday and the banks being closed, Polkoski cashed our cheques for us, otherwise I'd have jumped in front of the nearest bus.

'Well, how does it feel to be a bloated plutocrat once again?' chortled Dennis, obviously happy for me.

'Terrific, mate,' I said, tucking the fiver I owed him into his top pocket. 'All thanks to you. And now I'm going to buy you a big fat drink to celebrate.'

His face fell. 'Oh . . . heck, I'm sorry, Russ, but I . . .'

I held up my hand. 'Say no more – you have a date with the divine Devina, it's sticking out a mile, dirty sod. Go to it, maybe I'll see you tonight?'

'Well . . . actually she's not working tonight, either . . . or tomorrow, and we . . .'

'Beautiful. Let me know when the wedding is.'

'Heck, I'm sorry, Russ . . .'

'You're kidding! Matter of fact, I'm expecting a call that the projector's broken down,' I fibbed. 'Have a ball or even a couple, I'll see you when I see you. Tell her I'm standing-by in case you drop dead.'

'Okay,' he laughed. 'See you.'

In a nebulous sort of gloom, with no destination in mind, I drove through the lashing rain and suddenly found myself at home. I looked at the house . . . and suddenly the steam went out of life. It looked bloody terrible.

The room was unbearable. Standing at the window, watching the garden fill up like a bathtub, I asked myself what the hell I was doing there . . . in that God-awful room, in that house, looking down on that depressing garden.

She'd done it to me, of course. She was glamour, wealth, style, luxury, to say nothing of quite exceptional company. And suddenly I yearned to be away from all this and among all that. With her.

Dare I call her?

Would she want to know?

Was she, at that moment, staring out of her window at the pelting rain, an empty week-end looming, wishing I'd phone?

What could be the harm?

The harm could be that she *wouldn't* want to know, that she'd make an excuse, be cool, embarrassed. That would make me even more depressed.

To heck with it, I wouldn't call. It was stupid, I had no right to be there. Face reality, Tobin – *this* is your life.

This? I took another good look at the room. To hell with it – I would call!

I plunged down the stairs, stuck four pence in the box and dialled, my heart thumping, hoping she wouldn't answer, praying she would.

Brr brr . . . brr brr . . . brr . . . brr . . . brr . . . brr . . . thank God, she was out.

'Hello?' answered a female voice.

I jerked the receiver back to my ear. 'Gerta?'

'No, Mrs Gotlieb iss not here. Who iss calling, pliss?'

'I . . .' Careful, Tobin, careful. 'Who am I speaking to, please?'

'Zis iss her daily help, Hannah Klaus. May I take a message, pliss?'

'What time will Mrs Gotlieb be back, Hannah?'

'Who iss calling, pliss?'

Oh, blimey, we could go on like this for a fortnight.

'My name is Tobin . . . I'm a representative of Zip Electrics. I'm phoning to find out if Mrs Gotlieb has had any problems with her film projector.'

'Oh. Well, I'm afraid Mrs Gotlieb has gone away for a few days . . . perhaps a week. I don't know when she'll be back.'

My spirits nose-dived into the carpet. 'Oh. Thank you very much.'

I dropped the receiver into the cradle, my misery complete. Or so I thought.

Feet thundered down the stairs.

' 'Ello, 'ello, 'ello . . . and what do we have here – a bloke that's just lost a tenner and found a tanner? What's the matter, Tobin, is she pregnant? Serves you bleedin' right.'

Just the company I needed for the week-end – Frank The Fink Harris.

'Here, I've got just the story to cheer you up, Tobin. A bloke rushes into a chemist's shop and says to the bird behind the counter, "I want a packet of Durex and a solution of hydropolychlorodine mixed with *exactly* two parts of chloropolyhydrodine." And she says, "What d'you want the Durex for?" Ha ha ha . . . What d'you want the *Durex* for . . !'

'Frank.'

'Yes, mate?'

'Fuck off.'

Well, that was it – she'd scarpered. And why shouldn't she? She was free to do what she liked. I had to laugh . . . all that talk about Hollywood. Well, it was fun while it lasted.

Back to earth, son, I thought, again staring out of the window. And then I thought – are you going to stand here staring out of this window all bleeding week-end? Go on, get moving. You've got money in your pocket, get up West and see a flick, have a drink, feed the ducks in St James's park if they're not all drowned, but do *something*.

I did go up West. I did see a flick. I did have a drink. And it certainly did the trick. By the time I got back to the house, about ten that night, I was feeling terrific.

One thing about the Tobins, they don't stay down for long. Hit 'em with disappointment, crush 'em with despair, and they bounce back like rubber balls for more.

Happy to be home in my own environment, I climbed the rickety stairs and entered my ten-by-ten palace, my life once more slotted back into comforting perspective.

'Ohhh . . . *GAWD* . . !!' I cried, hurling my saturated raincoat at the wardrobe.

I kicked off my squelching shoes, ripped off my tie, turned to chuck it at the dressing table mirror . . . and then I saw it.

It was a long envelope, propped against the mirror. What-ho, I thought, I'm being sued.

I advanced on it, now seeing it had been delivered by hand, the handwriting bold and unfamiliar. Puzzled, I tore it open and pulled out a single sheet of notepaper, excitement surging through me as I read the signature.

Quickly lighting a fag, I sat on the bed, skimmed the page hurriedly, then began at the beginning, slowly. I read:

'Dear Russ,

After you'd gone last night I did a crazy thing. Unable to sleep, I got out the car and drove to Balham to see where you lived. I wanted to remind myself what a boarding house looked like. They haven't changed.

Once upon a time I knew a young girl who lived in such a house, then one day a fairy godfather came along and rescued her.

We all need a little help from a magic wand at least once in our lives. The enclosed is no guarantee of happiness, but perhaps it will ease the way to it.

I'm going away for a while. I have discovered this morning that the walls around me do indeed have eyes and I must escape them until it's over. Believe me, this has nothing whatever to do with our lovely evening. How could it?

You will be busy now, earning your part of the arrangement, which I'm sure you'll keep. Stay in touch, let me know what fate and fortune befall you, I will be most interested.

And perhaps one day you will report it to me first-hand. I would like that very much.

Be happy,

G.'

I stared at it, then picked up the envelope, almost afraid to hope what lay inside.

I stuck two fingers in it and pulled out the enclosure, the blue and red motif of British Airways bringing a flush of blood to my face. It couldn't be . . . but it damn-well was!

An open-dated single ticket to Los Angeles, USA!

I gaped at it, opened it, and a slip of paper fell into my lap. On it were the names and addresses of two people – a Mr Frank Sneider and a Mrs Genevieve Holmeyer – both of Hollywood, California. Under their addresses was a note from Gerta, 'See them – they will know who you are.'

I continued to stare – at the ticket, at the letter, at the note . . . it couldn't be true. It could *not* be true!

I got off the bed and paced the room, ground out my cigarette in the ashtray, lit another, paced some more . . . my brain boiling with shock, hope, ideas and excitement. It was crazy . . . a joke. I snatched up the airline ticket and devoured its details . . . London/Los Angeles via New York . . . it was written right there in ballpoint pen.

I let go a laugh, hit myself on the head, kissed the ticket, and took a flying header onto the bed . . . bounced on it like a trampoline. The crazy, beautiful, wonderful, fantastic woman . . . she'd actually done it!

I became quite still.

My part of the arrangement was . . . to earn five hundred pounds.

The problem sobered me . . . but in the next moment fired me with determination to do it – *and* as quickly as possible. Gerta had made me a gift of an opportunity of a life-time and I was damned if I'd let her down.

Five . . . hundred . . . pounds.

So little and yet, in my position, so very much.

Damn those deductions. I'd grossed a hundred and ten this week. Five weeks like this and I could have been away – but for those damned deductions.

Well, there was only one thing for it – I'd have to earn *two* hundred quid a week!

Could I do it?

Did I do it?

Did I get to Hollywood and look up Mr Frank Sneider and Mrs Genevieve Holmeyer?

I'll let you know next time I write.
All right?
Tarra.

GENERAL NON-FICTION

0426 Tandem

162560	Gerty Agoston **MY BED IS NOT FOR SLEEPING**	50p*
162641	**MY CARNAL CONFESSION**	50p*
175824	Nigel Balchin **THE BORGIA TESTAMENT**	60p
175905	**THE SMALL BACK ROOM**	60p
176030	**MINE OWN EXECUTIONER**	60p
176111	**A SORT OF TRAITORS**	60p
180593	Bill Bavin **THE DESTRUCTIVE VICE**	75p
152026	Aubrey Burgoyne **THE AMAZONS**	45p
163796	Catherine Cookson **THE GARMENT**	60p
163524	**HANNAH MASSEY**	60p
163605	**SLINKY JANE**	60p
162803	Jean Francis **COMING AGAIN**	45p*
151496	Joe Green **HOUSE OF PLEASURE**	50p*
165209	Brian Hayles **SPRING AT BROOKFIELD**	50p
172167	Harrison James **ABDUCTION**	50p*
135148	**COMING MY WAY?**	45p
150937	**HAVE IT YOUR WAY**	45p
045386	Olle Lansberg **DEAR JOHN**	40p
151577	Julie Lawrence **BLONDES DON'T HAVE ALL THE FUN!**	50p
16539X	Keith Miles **AMBRIDGE SUMMER**	50p
171446	Jack Millmay **REVELATIONS OF AN ART MASTER**	50p
16248X	Ingeborg Pertwee **TOGETHER**	50p
178815	Betty Smith **JOY IN THE MORNING**	70p*
179455	**MAGGIE: NOW**	75p*
178734	**TOMORROW WILL BE BETTER**	70p*
151224	Joannie Winters **HOUSE OF DESIRE**	50p*

0446 Warner/Wyndham

597724	Alex Cord **SANDSONG**	60p†
799416	Annabel Erwin **LILIANE**	95p

*Not for sale in Canada.

HUMOUR

0352	Star	
	Woody Allen	
300698	**GETTING EVEN**	50p*
	Alida Baxter	
398973	**FLAT ON MY BACK**	50p
397187	**OUT ON MY EAR**	60p
397101	**UP TO MY NECK**	50p
	Les Dawson	
397632	**THE SPY WHO CAME**	50p
	Alex Duncan	
397020	**VETS IN THE BELFRY**	50p
398612	**IT'S A VET'S LIFE**	60p
398795	**THE VET HAS NINE LIVES**	50p
	David Dawson	
396245	**VET IN DOWNLAND**	60p
	Stephen John	
397535	**WHAT A WAY TO GO!** (see also Tandem General Fiction)	50p
	King Kong	
397314	**MY SIDE**	60p
	Spike Milligan	
397780	**THE GREAT McGONAGALL SCRAPBOOK**	75p
	Jack Millmay	
397527	**REVELATIONS FROM THE RAG TRADE** (See also Tandem General Fiction)	50p
	Stanley Morgan	
396237	**INSIDE ALBERT SHIFTY**	70p
398965	**RUSS TOBIN'S BEDSIDE GUIDE TO SMOOTHER SEDUCTION**	60p
397454	**SKY-JACKED**	60p
	Harry Secombe	
396954	**GOON FOR LUNCH**	60p
	Keith Waterhouse	
396148	**MONDAYS, THURSDAYS (NF)**	60p
0426	Tandem	
	Tony Blackburn	
158350	**A LAUGH IN EVERY POCKET**	40p
136616	**DARLING – YOU ARE A DEVIL!**	50p*
	Spike Milligan	
157710	**THE BEDSIDE MILLIGAN**	35p
157982	**A BOOK OF BITS OR A BIT OF A BOOK**	35p
15827X	**A DUSTBIN OF MILLIGAN**	35p
158199	**THE LITTLE POT BOILER**	35p
	Spike Milligan & John Antrobus	
158008	**THE BED-SITTING ROOM**	35p

*Not for sale in Canada.